LITTLE OUTSIDE-IN-THE-SNOW
& OTHER FAIRY TALES

David Boyle has been writing about new ideas for more than a quarter of a century. He is co-director of the New Weather Institute, policy director of Radix UK, sa fellow of the New Economics Foundation, has stood for Parliament and is a former independent reviewer for the Cabinet Office. He is the author *of Alan Turing, Scandal* and *Before Enigma*, as well as a range of other books and stories. He lives in the South Downs.

Little
Outside-in-the-Snow

and other fairy tales

David Boyle

THE REAL PRESS
www.therealpress.co.uk

Published in 2020 by the Real Press.
www.therealpress.co.uk © David Boyle

ISBN (print) 9781912119196
ISBN (ebooks) 9781912119189

To Katy, with love

Chapters

Preface and acknowledgements

The term 'fairy tales' is a strange one – most fairy tales have no fairies in them. In fact, there is only one in any of these stories ('Loch Nowhere'). Yet there is something, I hope, of the same earthy simplicity in these tales, the same sense of magic and the same feeling that we have slipped into a parallel world that people feel from fairies.

The great Distributist poet G. K. Chesterton used to say that, once formal religion had disappeared, people would not believe nothing – they would start believing absolutely anything.

I have managed to avoid believing either in reincarnation or UFOs, perhaps because I remain a member of the Church of England – but I may well be the only policy wonk in the UK to believe in fairies.

I explain some of this in the final essay in this book, which was first published by *Bloom* magazine, based on a slightly longer version from *The Idler* (Boyle (2008), 'A bit of magic', Issue 41, Summer).

Thank you first to Carol Cornish, whose Writing

Space first got me writing stories like this – she quite literally changed my life.

Otherwise, 'Princess of the pictures' was written during a stay in the equally magical southern French town of Avène – where the waters cure people of eczema.

'Merlin', 'Puss' and 'Loch Nowhere' were published first in three books of modern folk tales from the New Weather thinktank (successively in *There was a knock at the door* (2016), *Knock Twice (2017)* and *Knock Three Times (2019)*, all edited by Andrew Simms, Steyning: New Weather/The Real Press).

'Basingstoke' was modelled on something very similar that happened to an ancestor of mine.

As for 'Lost', that was a story that forms a kind of *denouement* in my fairy novel *Leaves the World to Darkness* (2007, Steyning, the Real Press and also now as a kindle edition from Sharpe Books, London).

I hope you enjoy them and that the lack of fairies is made up by the wise men and women everywhere, and the hints of other tales – from the Grimm classics through to the less grim Washington Irving and William Morris.

A very gratefully acknowledge these people's help and inspiration too – and whichever sprite took the word 'fairies' out of the manuscript of this book – thank you for making me take a bit more care. The continuing mistakes were all mine...

David Boyle, Steyning, Autumn 2020

Little Outside-in-the-Snow

Once there was a neat and tidy kingdom, light years away from here, but very similar – where potatoes fell from the trees like blossom and white apples grew in the depths of the earth. At the heart of the kingdom was a city decked with flowers with neatly trimmed lawns and undignified hovels side by side. And at the heart of the city was a castle, beautifully designed and polished every morning by hundreds of carefully-trained servants.

In the daytime, the castle shone in the sunlight; in the night its pointed towers cast long shadows through the town. The king and queen were powerful and known throughout the world for their spectacular ceremonies, their carefully planned receptions and intricately detailed foreign policies. Nothing was left to chance and the few things that simply had to be – life being what it is – were covered by hefty insurance, paid for with an extra tax on the countryside. Their twelve children were well-known too: six princes and six princesses, handsome and beautiful.

One day, to her astonishment, the queen became pregnant again. She and her husband had planned to have exactly twelve children and then stop. In a rage, she summoned her doctors to demand an explanation for what had happened. They seemed irritatingly unwilling to provide one, but the queen's fury was nothing to the king's. "How dare you!" yelled the king, as soon as they were alone. "I was very careful to specify exactly the number of children we should have and you seem intent on flying in the face of my wishes."

"I assure you," said the queen. "I am entirely blameless in this. I simply follow your instructions from moment to moment. This is clearly your miscalculation." And she stormed off and locked herself into the West Wing for nine months.

It was winter before the door to her bed chamber opened again, and the snow was lying flat across the city, white under the moonlight, before it was brushed away in the morning by palace servants. After nine months, the palace women had barely managed to calm the queen at all. She stood at the door and shouted to her husband.

"Now what?" she screamed. Her voice and the faint sound of a new baby crying mingled in the stone corridors, making the suits of armour quiver in the Great Hall. "You deal with the problem. I'm going abroad to rest!" She left the baby behind, red-faced, frightened and alone with the women of her chamber. The Lord Chamberlain came and stared – from a safe distance – and went away again, scratching his head. So did the Chancellor and the cardinals of the court. Finally the king arrived, and stared into the room with a face like thunder. "It's no good," he said, with exasperation. "I will not have thirteen children. She'll have to go. Put her outside."

The palace staff nodded their heads gravely. Disagreement was untidy and they shared the king's conviction that twelve princes and princesses were quite enough – as, indeed, they shared all the king's convictions. There were the national finances to consider, the civil list, the dowries, the complications. The king was right, even if it was snowing.

It was left to the nurse to gather up the tiny princess, wrap her in a sheepskin and leave her outside the castle walls. With tears streaming down her face, because she knew she had to obey, she carried the princess down the long stone passages, past the bacon sizzling on the spit, past the armour and tapestries and the dozing sentries, down the drawbridge and into the streets.

Fresh snow was lying heavy on the ground and a sharp icy wind cut into the nurse's face as she clutched the princess to her breast. "If I leave her here, she'll be dead in an hour," she said to herself.

She knew no-one outside the palace, and when she approached likely looking women with the hope of fostering the child, they took one fearful glance at the bundle in its rich sheepskin, gathered their dirty rags about their faces and ran. Exhausted and frightened, the nurse remembered a small cleft in the battlements, away from the cold wind, she had seen decades before when she first arrived at the castle. She clambered up over the tufts of grass, rubble and discarded food and pushed past the bracken.

It was dry and, yes, it was almost warm. With her heart beating in her throat, she put the princess down gently, fed her a final bottle of milk, and with many backward glances, and tears rolling down her cheeks, she climbed back across the bridge, under the portcullis and into the palace. She was back an hour later, and as the sky darkened and the snow whistled outside, she sat in the small hole in the walls, and lulled the abandoned princess to sleep – the words of her lullaby mingling with the tearing wind.

She returned in the morning, and again and again, feeding her, soothing her when she could. Then a few days later, disaster struck. The nurse had caught a chill in her winter wanderings, and she fainted over breakfast.

She was carried to bed and, for three days, she lay delirious in a fever. When she came to it was early evening and a few minutes went by before she suddenly remembered the child. In terror, she dressed, ignoring the horrified remonstrations of her fellow servants and dashed down to the cleft in the walls which she had come to know so well. There could be no chance, could there – she asked herself as she ran – that the little princess could have survived even one day and one night in the snow without food? A terrible curse seemed to hover over her head.

But when her eyes adjusted to the dark, she could barely believe the sight. And yet, there was no doubt. Four eyes looked up at her, instead of two. The baby now lay next to the determined piercing eyes of a dark-haired vixen, a fox from the wintry streets, which had been driven by whatever impulse to take shelter and save the life of a fellow outcast. The nurse tiptoed away.

As the weeks passed and then months, she found it wasn't just the vixen which fed the princess, but crows bringing grubs or hedgehogs being nettle leaves to supplement the milk and porridge and love which the old nurse slipped with her away from the palace. When any of their shapes blocked the light as they appeared in the princess' hole in the wall, the baby's face would brighten in recognition. And on very special days, they would leave behind one of the glowing white apples from deep in the ground.

In the years that followed, she learned to smile, to talk, to play with the ragged children around the slopes of the castle, to pick through the palace rubbish, to laugh and to cry. The nurse brought her the school books discarded by her older brothers and sisters. But the burden of living such an existence in the hinterland of society took its toll: there were moments when the nurse could see a shadow passing across the face of her protégé.

When she was old enough, the nurse began plotting to bring her safely back into the palace as one of the servants. When the Chamberlain of the Household had finally agreed to hiring another scullery maid, she leapt for joy and dashed to where she knew the princess would be. "At last! At last!" she shouted excitedly, clutching the princess to her large bosom, where once she had held her tight that first wintry night. "At last you can come and live warm and safe with me, and be clothed and never have an empty belly."

But the princess looked sadly back at her in her torn and filthy clothes. "I cannot come," she said. "For I am Little Outside-in-the-Snow, and I must stay where I belong."

"But... But...," said the nurse, her words bunching hopelessly in her throat. "But you can't stay here. What will become of you? Just because you began here doesn't mean you always have to be here." But the princess was adamant and wouldn't say another word.

And in the years that followed, the nurse repeated her demand time and again. Offers of greater roles in the big house came and were sadly dismissed. Distant relatives of the nurse offered her places to live. The shoemaker down the rutted track in the town even proposed to her. But she simply smiled quietly, looked them in the eyes, brushing her golden hair away from her face and said: "I am Little Outside-in-the-Snow and I must stay where I belong."

But great events were beginning to unfold in the castle above. A prince from a neighbouring kingdom, of ineffable breeding, enormous wealth and astonishing learning had agreed to visit the palace and marry the princess of his choice. His one flaw was a fleeting indecision: he had managed to survive for four decades without choosing a wife.

"And he's so handsome too," whispered the serving girls and the princesses separately as he leapt down from his horse in the courtyard, his boots rattling on the cobbles. "He is a little unkempt, though," said the king. "He never seems to comb his hair."

"Well, I don't like this princess-of-his-choice business at all," complained the queen. "It's most untidy. We should have decided for him."

Needless to say, the official reception was a neat, sumptuous affair, planned down to the last detail. Not a feather on the plumes of the guards blew out of place. Not a sash clashed on the waists of the princesses. The prince was delightfully polite, kissing the hand of each princess in turn – "So unhygienic," said the queen in an undertone. With each one in turn he talked happily, he rode with each in the deer park and caressed each one lightly on the forearm. But at the end of the week, his expression had become fixed and his demeanour haggard.

"They are absolutely lovely," he told the king at the end of the week. "They do you credit. But I haven't been completely open with you." The prince told him that a wise man, much consulted in his own family, had urged him to marry one of the princesses specifically. He had conjured a picture of her, wild and beautiful, in the kind of clothes princesses rarely wear – dowdy, smelly even – but in her eyes shone a light and excitement and wonder and care and power which sent a shiver from the top of his coronet to the tips of his jewelled shoes.

"That fact is," said the prince uncomfortably, "none of your daughters seem to be the one. I don't want to be difficult, but – are you sure you have no other female children, who may have slipped your mind in the excitement?"

"Extraordinary idea!" said the king, though a

strange doubt had crept into his mind, which he instantly suppressed. "We don't behave like that in this country."

Alone again in his bed chamber, the prince was confused and disillusioned, doubting his own judgement, fearful of returning home without the longed-for alliance of love stoked and power broked. Then there was a muffled knock at the door. It was the old nurse.

She had overheard his audience with the king and knew immediately what she must do. Bowing slightly, she put her finger to her lips and – in the most servile way she could think of – motioned the prince to follow. In stockinged feet, they crept out of the palace and into the warm evening air. The children were playing and the last crickets were buzzing in the distance.

When he reached the cleft in the walls and saw the forgotten princess, he was overjoyed. Here was the wild royal beauty he had travelled for so long to find. In his excitement he kissed the old nurse and held out his hands. Nobody spoke. Then the princess drew herself up, threw off a few of her dirty rags and looked right up into his face, imperiously as if he was his equal, and – her eyes blazing – gently took his hands. The prince visited the cleft in the walls again the next day, and again the day after and then through the night they wandered along the moat, glinting in the starlight, hand in hand.

"You are my princess," he told her as the dawn seeped into the sky. "Come back to the palace, claim your birthright and let me marry you, cover you with gold and make you my queen. Let me love you until you are old and wise and wizened and beyond. Let me stroke your hair in the mornings and bathe you in the evenings. Let me kiss your eyes, and tend you in your dark hours of confinement and lift you up in front of the world. Let me draw you into my dreams."

"But alas, I cannot," said the princess sadly. "For I am Little Outside-in-the-Snow, and I must stay where I belong."

The prince was aghast. "Snow?" he said. "What snow? And I know exactly where you belong." But once again, the princess was adamant. He cajoled her through the night, pleaded through the following day – while the royal family in the castle above made anxious enquiries about his whereabouts – but it was no use. He returned to his room with its fine wall-hangings and fire in the grate and collapsed onto his bed in despair. He changed his clothes and, seeing nobody, left immediately for his arduous journey home.

"You cannot change where she belongs," said the old wizard months later. "You cannot change where anybody belongs. You have to change something else." He stroked his beard. "And if you change something else, you have to change everything. You have to pluck one of the white apples of the moon."

"What do you mean?" asked the prince nervously. But he loved the princess, so if he had to pluck an apple to win her, no matter how deep it was buried, then that was what he would do.

"Go down the cave at the foot of the Great Mountain," said the wizard. "And when the light fades, so they say, you will meet an old man who will guide you. But beware, prince! If you are whole-hearted in your desire; if you have no doubts in your mind about your quest, then you will win through. If not then you will be torn into little pieces."

"This apple-plucking business," asked the prince quietly. "How many have succeeded before me?"

"None at all," said the wizard, sweeping his robes behind him.

The prince gulped and examined his mind, fleetingly at first and then in great detail. He wandered the royal potato trees in the days that followed, with the sun on his face and potatoes in his hand and – sure enough – whenever his mind wandered, he had doubts. Maybe some even more wonderful princess would emerge later. Why should he go through this demeaning ordeal for an outcast in rags? If he remained single, he could have whichever women he desired.

But still the eyes of the princess burned inside his

head and he knew that, whatever risks lay ahead, he would have to try. He stayed awake that night in vigil before setting out. As the light arrived, he took one last look around his bedroom – his home since boyhood – etching the princess on his mind, saying goodbye to favourite hairbrushes, nick-nacks and suits. Then he strode out to meet his fate deep in the earth.

The cave was easy to find. And sure enough, as the light disappeared, an old man in a long white robe became suddenly visible. He greeted the prince by name. Bones were littered disconcertingly at his feet. For what seemed like weeks, lit only by a series of blazing torches, the prince followed the old man deep into the earth.

They passed through narrow paths in the rock, through vast caverns as big as the Great Hall in his father's palace, stalactites like tall spindly mountains, rock waterfalls like the raging ocean, strange creatures with great teeth and claws sleeping in their lairs, men without eyes eating worms in the dust. Yet every step of the way, he thought of her. Every pace brought some new facet of her, some new wisp of her hair remembered, before his mind.

"I must leave you here," said his guide at the entrance to the blackest cave. "We are nearly at the centre of the world. If you are pure in what you seek, you will win. If not, I fear you will never see the day again. Go through this tunnel and you will see a sword and a gnarled old tree, and the white apples of the moon growing there. Use the sword to pluck an apple – just one, mind – and you will win through, achieve your dream and turn the whole world inside out."

The prince was too frightened to speak, but he knew that any doubts he had would threaten his whole mission if he allowed them the space to breathe. So thinking of the Princess Outside-in-the-Snow, he plunged ahead. A hundred yards of pitch blackness, and the corridor ended, and his flailing hands came up against cold rock. He felt around to his right, then his left, and – yes! – there was the pummel of a sword. He lifted it and swept it through the air, and immediately a dull white light filled the cavern, and to his horror, he could see lying about him, the bones and armour of the heroes who had come before him and failed.

The rock was almost blue. It had red lines, like veins, across it and seemed to pulsate, like the beating heart of the world. It was covered in scars from the failed blows of forgotten adventurers. It beat with implacable cruelty. And growing out of it was the tree, as old as time itself. A tree wiser and deeper than any he had imagined, and hanging from its branches, glowing in what seemed like moonlight, were the apples – strange and forbidden and throbbing with light like the moon on a winter's night.

The prince raised the sword, then lost his nerve for a second. Was his heart pure? He raised it again, and for a second time he doubted himself. His 40 years slipped quickly through his mind: every cruelty of his own, every harsh word, every betrayal crowed into his ear. Then finally the pure sharp picture of the Little Princess Outside-in-the-Snow, her dignity and beauty and how much he loved her, and he raised the sword a third time. The cave seemed to vibrate in expectation. And, holding his hand underneath the nearest apple, he swung the sword round to separate it from the branch.

There was dead silence for a moment as the apple fell into his hand, then in the very distance, the prince could hear the sound of cries of loss, of cutlery and plates collapsing on the floor, of cows leaping over fences, of lovers succumbing after years of resistance, of books falling from shelves – all opening as they fell at pages of great significance which nobody had ever read – of portraits coming to life, of weapons melting in the hands of warriors. Then there was another sound, not heard through the ear, of growing. Of daffodils opening, of snow melting, of eggs cracking open, of the long forgotten seeds buried with the pharaohs beginning to burst into life.

With his guide, as solemn as before, he made his way out of the long cavern, back to the foot of the Great Mountain and he was hit by the tangy whiff of spring.

For two weeks he rode, through upturned valleys and hills overthrown, to the country of the princess, and every hour he went by, he checked the glowing apple which he carried next to his heart. By the time he arrived, unkempt and smelling, barely able to see between his aching eyelids, he could see that it had changed enormously. People seemed disorientated, happy-looking cows wandered in the streets, furniture was piled in front gardens while flowers bloomed in the carpets through the open windows. But as he approached the castle he woke completely, and stopped still in astonishment. The chandeliers, wallpaper and weapons seemed attached to the outside walls. Baths hung from the sides. Portraits glinted in the sunshine. Suits of empty armour and the antlers of long-dead stags protruded into the town.

He walked up the drawbridge, which now seemed to be lifting up inside the castle itself. There was no sign of the guards – still less the royal family – and the walls inside the castle were weatherbeaten and rough, and the sunlight shone in through the roof. Some cats were playing where the throne room had stood. A vixen and her cubs preened themselves in pride of place, as if they owned the palace themselves. The potato trees had disappeared and in their place stretched new orchards down the corridors and in the bedrooms. And there in the very heart of the inverted castle, dressed in fine clothes, with the light glinting in her hair and the swallows circling her head like a crown, was the princess – smiling with delight.

She leapt up when she saw him and he ran towards her, pulling off his leather gloves as he ran and holding out the white apple. "Well," he said, as he took her in her arms. "If it isn't Little Princess Inside-in-the Snow."

Puss

Once there was a miller who lived rather longer than his allotted three score years and ten, and who had three great-grandchildren (he had more, actually, but they had long since emigrated).

When he died, well past his hundredth year, he had become muddled about the true values of the world, or so it was said. He left his milling premises to his eldest great-grandchild, who knocked it down and developed it into flats for wealthy far eastern investors. He left his business to his next great-grandchild who had stopped actually milling flour some decades before and was simply buying and selling wheat futures.

To his youngest and favourite great-grandchild, he left his cat, to which he had been much attached in his declining years.

This youngest was called Rachel – but everyone called her Dickie – and she was a little miffed by it. When the family solicitor handed over the cat, after signing a number of forms, Dickie took it home to her flat in Crystal Palace and stared sadly at it – wondering what would become of them both.

'Don't worry,' said the cat, cleaning its paw. 'I can arrange things that will make everything perfect, and I can do so far better than the Ugly Brothers.'

'You mean *my* brothers? My brothers aren't ugly. On one of them was even featured in GQ. Hold on...'

Dickie had suddenly realised that the cat had spoken to her.

'Do that again, can you?

'Do what?'

'You know... Say something?'

'I just did. If you mean it is strange to find a cat that talks, I have to admit that my fellow moggies leave something to be desired in the human stakes.'

'You *can* talk. How? I mean, how is it possible?'

'Well, your great-grandfather, whose acquaintance I was honoured to make for some years, did talk to me a great deal. He helped me, you know. It makes a difference.'

'Even so, I'm not sure that even a talking cat can get me out of my current mess. There is no way I can pay my rent this month. I had been counting on a small legacy to...' Dickie burst into tears.

'Come on now, cheer up. I may just be a cat, but I'm a human one. If you're loved – I mean properly, you know – then you become human. And your great-grandfather really loved me. As he did you.'

'I know, I know. But love just isn't enough when it comes to paying the rent, I'm afraid.'

'Alright. We will see about that,' said Puss. 'Pass me my boots, just there on the side. Who do you owe the rent to?'

'Your boots? This is getting silly. Well, it's a company called Grunt and Grunt, letting agents. But they are only...'

It was too late. Puss had gone.

'Excuse me,' said the cat. 'May I speak to Mr Grunt?'

'Mr Grunt has retired and sold the business. Did you have an appointment?'

'No, but I represent Dickie Miller, you know – the film star? You don't. Where have you spent the last few years? She's very interested in renting in Crystal Palace. I was wondering whether you had any properties there.'

'Hold on. The managing partner is now Mr Ugh, and I believe he may be free...'

But once more, the cat had gone.

Mr Ugh unfortunately was barely able to string two words together, and he spent much of the meeting searching unsuccessfully for Dickie Miller on his mobile phone. But the mention of a thousand pounds a week seemed to interest him strangely. And he agreed to discuss with a tenant in just such a property, who he implied could easily make way.

Puss said there was a condition. He needed to meet the ultimate owner of the building.

This disturbed Mr Ugh, or at least that is what he seemed to be trying to express. But it wasn't long before Puss left the office with the address of a property company in the City of London.

'We do try to keep the clients out of the somewhat messy business of actually renting,' said Ms Vanessa St Hilda-Pinstripe, the managing director of sales. 'I hope you understand, this request is somewhat untoward. But I am familiar with the work of Dickie Miller. She is beautiful, isn't she? In fact, I saw her last time I crossed the Atlantic in *Blah Blah Land*, such a good film. So I am willing to make an exception. I will contact Mr – oh gosh...'

In a jiffy, Puss had leapt over the desk and looked at her email, and seen who the client was – and was gone again, on its way up the river, speeding on a passing launch with the spray in its fur.

Puss stood outside a wonderful white painted mansion in Blackheath, with black window frames, and a cobbled courtyard beyond a huge pair of black gates. Now, finally, it pulled on its leather boots. This was the moment.

'Mr O'Gre's residence. Can I help you?' said the

intercom.

'I have come without an appointment on an important matter concerning the actress Dickie Miller,' said Puss.

'I'm afraid Mr O'Gre sees nobody without an introduction.'

'Oh, on the contrary, as I'm sure he will remember, Mr O'Gre shared a platform with her in Davos earlier in the year and invited her over. I am simply facilitating the meeting.'

'Oh very well, hold on and I will find out.'

There was a crunching, electronic noise and Puss waited fifteen minutes and, then slowly and inexorably, the great gates swung open and the cat was inside.

'I have very little time,' said Mr O'Gre. 'I have seen you partly because of Dickie, who I remember well, and partly because of what my PA told me had showed up on the security camera. I have never met a talking cat before.'

Puss bowed low.

'My mistress has a great yearning to get to know you better. We are tremendously grateful for your time. She is also a great supporter of your budget airline.'

Mr O'Gre preened himself a little. 'I know, I know. Oh excuse me, I only have five minutes. I have to give the go-ahead to a motorway through the rainforest somewhere or other. As she may also know, I run a jewellery brand and a railway franchise, and a number of businesses which I doubt you can afford to patronise.'

Puss sat himself humbly at the end of the desk. 'My mistress wants to ask you – how do you manage it all? I know your slogan implies it: 'Trust me, I'm an Ogre'. It manages to convey all the scintillating vitality of youth, does it not? But what about you, you can't possibly manage all these enterprises, can you? You can't know what's going on. I mean, how can you know this motorway won't make the greenhouse effect worse?'

'DATA!' barked Mr O'Gre. 'The data never lies. I therefore take every decision in every one of my businesses. I *can* be everywhere. Look at these figures pouring into my computer screen. The allow me to know everything. Data, data, data.'

'You are so right,' said Puss. 'You can't trust people to decide things. You have to know.'

'Data can do absolutely everything. It can help you eat better, it can regulate your heart beat. Right now it is telling me to eat another XZd45 pill to give me the basic necessities of life. Have you got a glass of water? Excuse me!' He rang a bell and through the house came the lone PA, her shoes echoing down the empty corridors, glaring somewhat, with a glass of water.

'Oh, I don't know,' said Puss after she had gone. 'You can't really change yourself with data can you?'

'Certainly I can. Look at this.'

Mr O'Gre took a deep breath and pressed a couple of buttons and, a moment later, he had transformed himself into a roaring lion. Puss hid behind the designer sofa which appeared to have been made out of a cow. Its intestines were showing.

'Careful of that thing. It's a Damien Hurst,' said Mr O'Gre, returning to his usual shape. 'It isn't pretty, but you should see what its worth.'

'Very impressive, but it's all very well,' asked Puss. 'Can you use your data to transform yourself into something small? You probably can't, can you?'

'You mean virtual reality? Of course I can,' said Mr O'Gre, fiddling with some buttons. A moment later he had become a mouse, scrabbling across the papers on his pristine desk.

Quick as a flash, Puss was on him and a moment later, had eaten him whole.

Licking the remains of Mr O'Gre from his lips, Puss told the PA that her boss had decided to leave quite quickly and had agreed to let the house immediately to his friend Dickie Miller, the actress.

'Honestly,' she said, with an air of resignation. 'That's just like him. Now I probably won't see him for years.'

The rest of the story, how Mr O'Gre turned out to have wired his business empire up to an algorithm that ran it without his human involvement, or anyone else's – how Rachel/Dickie moved in to his home – is all pretty well known.

So is the story of how Puss tricked the King of Hollywood into giving Rachel a complete set of the finest clothes and now she married his wastrel son – who she divorced in an extremely lucrative settlement some weeks later.

So indeed is the story of how she became Lord Mayor of London. That need not detain us now.

What may still be of interest, perhaps, is the conversation she and Puss had when he came back, picking out pieces of Mr O'Gre from his teeth.

'One thing I don't understand, Puss,' said Rachel/Dickie. 'You may have the shape of a cat, but you are really completely human aren't you? And yet Mr O'Gre, who was supposed to be human, had transformed himself into some kind of, well, *beast*? And as for my landlords at Grunt and Grunt, well – honestly...'

'Well,' said Puss, looking thoughtful. 'As I understand it, parents switch on the brains of babies when they look into their eyes and love them. Your great-grandfather really loved me, as I said. He loved me into being human. Unfortunately, too much exposure to data tends to have the opposite effect –

all those mechanical simplifications. The more Mr O'Gre exposed himself to screeds of numbers, thinking they described the world, the less human he became. As for Mr Ugh, well ...'

'Really? I can hardly believe it.'

'Ah well, don't just take my word for it. Look it up: Sullivan, Wilson and Sarro (2014), 'Maternal regulation of infant brain state'. It does rather change one's view of dumb beasts, doesn't it.'

Merlin and the small dog

"It's no use," Jack's mum sighed as he came in with Timothy, their cocker spaniel. "The miners have moved onto the site. There's nothing we can do."

For six months now, Jack's mum had signed petitions and written letters to the prime minister, trying to stop the other side of their hill from being turned into a big open cast coal mine.

"They can't have done," said Jack, taking off his coat. Timothy looked around for his dinner.

"They can and they have. There's nothing more to be done and, once they've dug up that side of the hill, they say they will dig up this side. We've done everything we can."

"Not our woods. They're ancient woods. Mr Murgatroyd said so."

"I'm afraid so, Jack," said his mum, looking tired and miserable. "We'll just have to move, though goodness knows where we can move to. What is that thing that Timothy's brought in?"

"Yuck," said Jack bending down. Timothy had

dropped a muddy looking bone at his feet. He was wagging his tail and looking pleased with himself.

"Oh, throw it out into the garden will you?" said Jack's mum. "He's brought quite enough mud just on his paws."

Jack loved the woods that stretched up the hill behind the estate. He loved living under the ancient hill – Merlin's Hill it was called – and he had begun over the years to feel that they were his woods. At least his and Timothy's. It was Jack's job every morning and evening to take Timothy for a walk there, and he hardly ever saw anyone else walking there.

The thought of having to move away, while the miners demolished the old hill bit by bit, was just awful. He threw Timothy's muddy bone out of the back door and settled down to his own dinner, miserable about the future – not just because he was sad, but because he could see his mum was so sad as well.

"I have to leave early tomorrow morning," said his mum. "I'm on the early shift. Can you take Timothy for his walk and then put him in the kitchen? I'm so sorry Jack, but you'll have to give yourself breakfast this time."

It poured with rain in the night. Jack was woken by his mum letting herself quietly out of the house at dawn and lay there thinking about their hill.

Then he dozed and only just managed to wake himself in time. He pulled on his school uniform, grabbed some toast and put Timothy on his lead. He peered outside the back door and caught sight of the muddy bone which Timothy had found the night before. It had been washed by the rain.

Strange. Jack peered closer. This was no ordinary bone. It seemed to have holes in it. He picked it up and ran it under the tap. It looked extremely old, but there was no doubt about it. It was carved as a whistle.

"Look what you found, Timothy. You are a clever dog. I wonder who lost this." Timothy wagged his tail.

On an impulse, Jack put the whistle to his lips and blew. A faint note sounded. He tried again. Some old mud blew out of the end. Finally, he opened the back door wide and blew with all his might.

To his surprise, a long low note came out. It shook the leaves in the tree in the next door garden and seemed to echo in the air. Then he remembered the time. He locked the door, picked up Timothy's lead, put his homework by the front door, and set off for the woods.

"Come on Timothy. I haven't got long this morning. I've got to be in school in fifteen minutes."

Once they were through the gate into the woods, he let Timothy run and he streaked ahead up the hill.

He could hear barking in the distance.

"The mining company must be starting already," he said to himself. "Timothy, come back! I have to go to school!"

Jack felt crosser and crosser as he ran uphill, along the slippery mud paths, after his dog. To his surprise, he found he still had Timothy's bone whistle. He blew it again furiously. At this rate, he was going to be very late. He looked behind him. He could no longer see the road or the estate.

At long last he could see Timothy ahead. As he got closer, Jack realised that he was not alone. Sitting on an old tree trunk, talking to Timothy, was an extremely old man with a very long white beard and a hat that made him look a little like Father Christmas. He appeared to be wearing a dirty leather dressing gown.

Jack was nervous of talking to people he didn't know and he stood and wondered what to say.

"Thank you for keeping my dog. I have to get to school," he said.

The old man turned to him crossly. He looked more wrinkled than anyone he had ever seen. "Who are you? Why have you called me?"

"I haven't called you," said Jack, feeling very confused.

"You called me. You called me twice. Nobody has called me for a very long time indeed. So tell me, has the dawn broken? Has the spring begun? Has history arrived again?" Jack stared at him.

"Don't stare, boy. You blew the whistle. You called me out of sleep. You did so twice."

"I'm sorry," said Jack pulling out the bone pipe. "Timothy brought me the whistle and I didn't know what it was. I can give it back. It isn't damaged or anything."

The old man held out his hand and took it. His hands were rough and bony and like the hands of an ancient badger.

"Nobody calls me by accident. You may not know the reason, but there is one. I know the world, boy. I may not have lived in it for a very long time, but I know its ways. What is your name?"

"Jack," said Jack trying to attract Timothy's attention. "I have to go to school."

"No doubt, no doubt. But there is a reason for this meeting. Nobody calls Merlin from out of the hill by mistake. Come with me, Jack. I will not keep you long. Follow me."

He rose as if he was a much younger man and, for the first time, Jack could see that he was standing next to what looked like a great iron gate in the side of the hill. It was standing open.

He was just explaining that his mother had always warned him not to go anywhere with strangers, when Timothy leapt up, barked twice and headed through the gates.

"It seems as if your dog knows the way," said Merlin, his eyes twinkling. "You have blown the whistle. You must see what you must see."

Jack was horrified and beginning to be scared. "Timothy!" he shouted into the tunnel. "Oh heavens..."

Merlin held the gate open. It creaked a little on his old hinges. Jack slipped inside calling for Timothy. Now he knew he was going to be late, but how could he leave his dog inside the old hill? He had no idea there was a gate. Why hadn't he seen it before?

The passage was very dark but straight, and it was lit by small glowing lamps.

"Glow worms," said Merlin. "Keep straight on until the very heart of the hill."

Their footsteps thumped on the hard mud floor. Occasionally a drip from the ceiling fell on Jack's head. In the distance, he could see an orange flicker which must have been from firelight. He felt himself shaking with fear. How stupid he was to have gone inside the hill. He might never get out again.

Finally, they were in a huge chamber. Jack could see a big fireplace with the flames gently licking around some logs. There was Timothy lying by the fire, looking a bit guilty.

"Timothy, you naughty dog. Come with me now,

will you. Thank you, Mr Merlin, but could you help me us find our way out now?"

"A moment with you first, my boy," said the old man, beckoning him over, and for the first time Jack turned round and saw a sight that just made him gasp. The cave was lit by burning torches along the walls. There seemed to be warriors asleep around the edge of the cave, all with long beards, glinting breastplates and swords beside them, covered in cloaks. They were dusty and some of them half covered in earth or by leather rugs. Behind them, Jack could see horses tethered in hay and weapons along the wall. Then opposite the fire, on the other side of the chamber, was a rough wooden chair and a man with a grey beard leaning heavily on the armrest. He also seemed to be fast asleep.

Jack pinched himself. The morning had been getting even odder, but he thought he must now be dreaming. Had he actually just stayed in bed? He desperately tried to wake himself up.

"Tell the king," said Merlin softly, indicating the sleeping greybeard. Jack could see a crown hung on the back of the throne. It was battered and needed a polish. The king himself was wreathed around with cobwebs. "Tell the king why you called me and then you may go, and you may take with you anything you see."

Merlin pointed next to the king, and Jack saw

piles of plates of gold and silver, great jewels and broaches and chests of money, like a pirate's treasure trove.

How could he tell him, Jack wondered to himself? He looked fast asleep.

But Timothy thought otherwise. He went up to the throne and sniffed loudly. Then he growled and let out a great bark.

"Timothy, no!" shouted Jack, dashing over and finally putting the dog on his lead, tugging him desperately away.

But it was too late. The sleeping king moved. His eyelids flickered. He looked about him blindly.

"Is it day?" he asked in a rough voice.

"No, sire, but this young man has brought us news from up above. Tell him, boy."

Then Jack had a brainwave. Of course he had news and anyone living in this hill would want to know it. "It's true, your majesty," he said, unsure how to address sleeping kings. "It is true. The men have come with machines and they are going to dig up the hill for coal."

Slowly the king became more alert, sitting up straight in his throne. Merlin got nearer as Jack told the story of the petitions and the plans by the miners and the big company which had bought their hill. He talked about global warming and fossil fuels. Still, the ancient king listened.

"It is true what he says, sire. Our hill is in danger."

"You have done well, young man," said the king. "I salute you and I reward you. Take from the table anything you can carry. Take it before my warriors awake. Take it with my blessing."

"Thank you, my lord," said Jack. "Come on Timothy."

He walked over to the table heaving with gold, seeing it through piles of cobwebs and dirt. At the front of the table was a short sword in a beautiful jewelled scabbard. He lifted it up, blew off the dust and began to pull it out of its sheath.

But as he did so, a low sound echoed around the chamber like the shaking in the air he heard when he first blew the whistle. A wind began to swirl among them, and the cobwebs began to blow away.

"Not the sword," shouted Merlin from the throne. "Not yet!"

Jack turned round to see the nearest warrior getting slowly to his feet, brushing the cobwebs away and blinking around him in the candlelight.

"Is it day?" he asked.

"No, no..." said Jack desperately, shutting the sword back into its ancient sheath and dropping it. "Go back to sleep."

All around him, the warriors seemed to be waking. He panicked, pulled Timothy close to him and ran from the room back down the passageway he had come from. As he ran, a voice echoed around him in whispers.

"Jack, Jack, Jack," it said. "If you had just drawn the sword and heard the horn, you would have been the happiest that was ever born."

Jack's feet echoed on the hard earth floor. Timothy's paws pattered next to him as they raced for the light in the distance.

There was the gate. Jack leapt through, scratching himself on the brambles growing round the entrance, which he hadn't seen before. Then he breathed a sigh of relief, raced down the hill as fast as he could go on the slope without letting go of the lead. Trees and bushes flashed by. Sometimes he skidded in the mud. He could hear his panting breath and only then remembered school. He was going to be at least half an hour late. He would have to explain to his teacher or he would be in trouble.

It took him ten minutes to get home, put Timothy in the kitchen with some food, and to change his muddy trousers and be back on the road to school with his homework under his arm.

The school gates were deserted. He had to ring the bell. His footsteps echoed through an empty school hall as he made his way to his classroom. As he walked, he tried to understand what had happened that morning, and tried to think of an excuse for being late.

The classroom door swung open.

"You're late, Jack," said his teacher.

"Yes, Mr Murgatroyd, I'm afraid I..."

"Yes, out with it? Do you have a note from your mother?"

"No, I..." The whole class was looking at him. He could see Neil and Robin giggling with each other. They were enjoying it.

"Jack, be so good as to inform us why you are late and then we can get on with what we were doing."

Jack stared at him.

"We're waiting," said Mr Murgatroyd.

There really was nothing for it. "Well, the truth is that something odd happened to me on my way to school and my dog ran away down a hole in the hill..."

"Your dog," said Mr Murgatroyd, blinking a little...

"Yes, and inside the hill was a sleeping king, surrounded by sleeping warriors and swords and shields and gold and he asked me if it was daytime, and I told him about the new coal mine, and then – well, I got scared, and a ran out and I had to change my trousers."

"Your trousers?"

"Yes."

There was half a minute's silence and then the class erupted. The laughter lasted so long that Jack even began to laugh himself.

Mr Murgatroyd looked more and more cross.

"You will go and see the head teacher and do so now," he said. "I will not be made a fool of in my own classroom. Sleeping kings and warriors. I ask you. Now go!"

"But really, Mr Murgatroyd. It's true. It really happened."

"Go. Get out of my sight.

Neil and Robin were waiting for him at break time. "You are an idiot, Jack. Where did you get that story from?"

As he walked past people from his class, they giggled at him. Within minutes the whole school seemed to know. There were jeers and pointing fingers. Jack hid himself away in the corner of the playground. Perhaps he wouldn't have believed the story himself. If only Timothy could talk, he would be able to tell people – but of course he couldn't. Perhaps it really had been some kind of dream.

It wasn't until they were back in the classroom, and Mr Murgatroyd had started on a lesson about France when he heard that familiar rumble – part horn, part shaking – that he had heard inside the cave. Nobody else seemed to have heard it. But a few minutes later there was the sound like horses hooves in the road outside.

"Please, Mr Murgatroyd," said Jasmine urgently from beside the classroom window that overlooked the road. "There is something going on outside."

"Ignore it please, Jasmine."

The noise got louder, as if horses were racing past the school gates. More and more, they could only think about the noise from outside. Finally, Mr Murgatroyd walked over to the window. Then he stood still and stared.

"I don't believe it," he said. "Class, stay seated."

But it was too late. Everyone in the class was crowding round the window and staring. Jack could hardly see past them.

"What is it? What is it?" said those children who could not push their way through.

Then the head teacher was at the door. "Mr Murgatroyd, there seems to be some kind of disturbance outside. I don't quite understand it. There are some people dressed as warriors riding down the street, and looking – I must say – extremely realistic."

"I can see. I can see," he said. "Jack, come here a moment."

Jack pushed through the crowd of silent children. There were his warriors, mounted on warhorses, galloping between the parked cars in School Road, with armed with swords and daggers. Streamers fluttered from the end of their spears. Their beards swept along in the wind. The tails of their horses swished in the air and their leather shields were clipped behind them. Then came the horns again. The air shook.

"Is that what you saw?"

"Yes," said Jack. "That was what I saw."

"Then I believe I owe you an apology. Any idea what they are doing here?"

Suddenly Jack did know. It came to him in a flash as he looked up towards the hill.

"I think they are heading to the mining site."

Mr Murgatroyd followed his gaze. They were indeed heading around the other side of the hill. And in a minute or two later they were out of sight.

There was silence for a few moments after they had gone. Jack noticed his classmates avoiding his eyes. There seemed nothing to say. Nobody mentioned it at lunchtime. It was as if the sight of warriors charging down their familiar street had been too odd to talk about.

The head teacher gave the class a short talk about how some things are too strange to talk about outside the school. "I hope you all understand," he said. They did seem to a few moments later, Mr Murgatroyd was back talking about France as if nothing had happened.

It was certainly very strange. Nobody mentioned the warriors to Jack again. They seemed to be embarrassed about it, as if they had all been dreaming and didn't want to say so. But later that day, the mining contractor's trucks and diggers began to drive away from the site.

"How extraordinary," said Jack's mum a week later, reading from the newspaper. "Listen to this. 'International Fossil Fuels PLC, who had been granted permission for their super-open cast coal mine, have now abandoned the site. They blame geological difficulties.'"

"Does that mean they're going?"

"It does. We won after all. Our old hill is saved."

""Does that mean we can go on living here?" asked Jack.

"Yes, darling," said his mum. "Incidentally, you never told me how you got so muddy in your school trousers last week. I just found them behind the washing basket. They were covered in thorns and cobwebs as well. I don't know how you managed it."

Jack thought about his warriors often. Many times, he came close to telling his mum about them, but he never did – but he did wonder about all that gold. Sometimes, taking Timothy for a walk, he would try to follow the path he had taken that morning, looking behind every bush and bramble for the rusty iron gate that he had walked through.

He could never find it.

Princess of the Pictures

Once there was a little village hidden away in a green valley, with a river rippling through it on one side and an old railway siding beside it on the other. The river rippled so slowly that, it was said, if you dropped a stick into it from the old stone bridge at one end of the village, it would take a week to arrive at the small wooden footbridge at the other end. The railway was almost as slow – or so it was said.

It was, as you can see, a beautiful village – really the most beautiful in the whole world according to the people who lived there – a strange and wary people, much given to disapproval.

They were right in a way too. "We have the most beautiful thatched roofs too," said M. Le Trésourier, who was hoping to be the mayor. "And the most beautiful birds, and – let's face it – the most beautiful cows too. I mean, look at that one! You see what I mean?"

"What we need is a beautiful princess to complete the scene," said his wife Claudine.

"Aren't the cows enough?" M. Le Trésourier was

apt to speak a little sharply to his wife – it was another habit in the village. "I don't know where we'll find a princess these days. Or do you have one stashed away somewhere?"

"No, my dear, I do not. Only we need something like that. If not a real princess, then someone who looks like a princess. You must admit, most of our neighbours are not exactly oil paintings."

M. Le Trésourier was thoughtful for a moment. He could see immediately the sense in what his wife said, but was determined not to let on.

"Pshaw! The very idea! I've never heard anything so ridiculous," he said, with some conviction.

Actually, M. Le Trésourier was thinking hard. They did need someone to raise the tone a little, didn't they? A May Queen or something similar. You can't be the most beautiful village in the world if absolutely everyone who lives there is as ugly as sin.

And, come to think of it, he did have someone in mind.

It was the little daughter of M. and Mme. Lapin, both schoolteachers, who were themselves minor celebrities in the village for their alleged blood relations with the local counts in the chateau on the hill.

And here lies the heart of our story, because their daughter Régine was no ordinary child at all. She might well have been beautiful; or she might not.

Nobody really knew, because since the age of seven – almost from the moment she had been given a bedroom of her own – Régine had refused to leave her room.

The Lapins reasoned with her outside the door for weeks – no for months, honestly – sometimes logical, sometimes demanding, sometimes just pleading, and in very extreme moments, very angry. These were very extreme moments because M. and Mme Lapin were never angry – they didn't believe in it, they said – it was just that very occasionally, they despaired of ever seeing their daughter again, and lost their temper. But when either of them did so, the other would be so shocked that they would go silent for the rest of the day and leave copies of books about the evils of rage lying around the house, open at pointedly relevant pages.

It was all to no avail. They left Régine's meals on a tray outside her bedroom door, and peered hopefully towards the French windows, with the curtains drawn, that marked her access to the garden.

But they also left hints for the neighbours, who were aware that Régine was no ordinary child, that her peculiarity lay not just in her behaviour, but in her extraordinary beauty. "Ah well, it's so difficult for her," they would sigh, as they watched the ducks fly in down the river for the night, and the darkness spread down the narrow streets. "It's so hard for her because of her gift."

"Her gift, yes," agreed M. Lapin, listening carefully, as if he had thought of it for the very first time.

The neighbours would nod their heads gravely, as if they believed it. Then they would walk slowly back indoors and agree that the Lapins had been too lax in their upbringing and that they didn't believe a word of these 'gifts'.

"All those fancy ideas! Her own bedroom at her age! Leading out into the garden, if you please! Why at her age, I was still sleeping on straw at the end of the stables. If I was given a sheet occasionally, I was very grateful, I can tell you."

Week in, week out, Régine would stay in her room, demanding things from her poor parents by writing on small pieces of paper and slipping them under the door.

"She wants another tube of ultramarine. Come on, come on, woman! I warned you we would run out," shouted M. Lapin in impatience – and Mme. Lapin would hurry out, whatever the time, a fetch her another tube of paint. Régine's work came first.

It nearly always was paints she demanded. Because Régine – young though she was – was determined to be an artist. And she churned the paintings out with a passion. Sometimes at dead of night, while the foxes wandered through their overgrown garden, the Lapins would hear the splash splash, scrape scrape noise, as their daughter set to with another canvas, another work of art. And they glowed with the special pride of parenthood.

"Your last picture showed real promise – the one with the green haystack," said Mme Lapin tentatively through the door one morning, in an attempt to strike up conversation.

"What do you know about it, Maman?" said Régine. "Just get the paint I asked for, OK?"

"And she's only eight!" said her mother proudly.

"Yes," said M. Lapin sadly. "If only she dealt with the garden with the same enthusiasm."

The one thing that upset Régine's father wasn't so much the enforced separation from his daughter – there were compensations about that, after all – but the fact that by barricading herself into what had originally been a guest bedroom some years before, she had also shut off the only access to the garden, which rapidly became packed with the most unusual trees, with just enough space between them for the most exotic butterflies to flit between them, and birds with songs nobody had heard for a century or more gathered happily in the branches.

Régine sat on her bed by her easel, reading books about girls with ponies and painting, painting, painting, staring out at the birds and smiling to herself, and deciding which finished canvasses she would next slip under the door.

"Haystacks! What a stupid idea!" she said out loud to herself. Because, as Maman really should have known, every last one of her paintings was of the same thing: herself.

They were, in short, all self-portraits. Sometimes the paintings were obviously of her, with her hair piled high on her head, or a multi-coloured blouse, and rosy cheeks. Sometimes they were as she imagined she would look like wearing blacksmith's overalls or armour, or as a fine lady with poodles, from the olden days. Sometimes they were more like approximations – experiments: what she might look like inside out, or in the dark, or when she was in the womb. When they were dry, they were slipped under the door and her parents framed the ones they liked the best. Régine could sometimes hear them pointing them out to neighbours, making sure they appreciated the use of colour and contrast, or the sharp lines and shading.

But she never came out. Her old friends, her favourite cousins came and went, but Régine stayed behind the door with the curtains over the French windows kept firmly drawn. "If they want to know me, they can look at my pictures," she said to herself, and she was pleased with the sound of it.

And so the years went by, and the grass grew even longer in the garden – it was sometimes now even hard for the butterflies to flit between the trees, hard even for the sound of the railway engine puffing by to filter through the undergrowth. M. and Mme. Lapin became fatter and more respected in their professional lives, and more and more proud of their daughter – the less they could recognise her, the more proud of her they were.

But Régine stayed put. She was 18 years old when M. Le Trésourier was having his conversation with his wife about princesses.

"Mon Petit Choux," said M. Le Trésourier to his wife, in a craven, wheedling voice. "I believe I have an idea. I know where we can find your princess. And I'll tell you where. It's that girl who never goes out. The one that paints."

"What do you mean? What a silly idea! She could look like the back of Bertrand the Bullock for all we know."

"That's the point, isn't it," said M. Le Trésourier, looking smug. "We don't know – and neither does anybody else. Nor will they. They will imagine it. Do you understand? And what they imagine will far surpass even the most beautiful princess we could ever lay our hands on. If you see what I mean," he said, with great delicacy.

So M. Le Trésourier set about spreading the rumour that, not only was theirs the most beautiful village in the whole wide world, but the most beautiful young lady lived there who ever lived anywhere – the beautiful, mysterious and elusive Régine – who, if not exactly a princess in the strict sense, was one of nature's true princesses, a princess to the roots of her hair and to the ends of her toenails."

The news began to spread, first to the nearest market town, where the farmers discussed her as they prodded their fat pigs at market, and then to the city, where the students and professors debated Régine's beauty and made up Latin epigrams about it. And then to the palace itself, where the king and queen mentioned the mysterious beauty in passing over breakfast one morning, before moving on to the subject of their own children.

It was inevitable that soon the visitors would start to arrive: the farmers' sons in search of wives from the town, the young bucks from the colleges, the merchants, the bakers, the furniture-makers, the young and the old, the printers, the sprinters, the hot and the cold – and they all made their way in hopeful ones and competing twos, down the slow railway to the village, just in dribbles and first and then in a flood.

M. and Mme Lapin moved away and employed an agent to look after the house and sell Régine's paintings of herself. M and Mme Trésourier built a fine guest house to accommodate all the visitors, and became rather wealthy and a little plump. He and his wife greeted them with a tricolour sash – even though he wasn't yet the mayor – and a handshake tough enough to remove a doorknob.

The money poured in. Soon the village shops were doing a powerful trade selling reproductions of Régine's more famous pictures, the little train was puffing itself hoarse and M. Le Trésourier was finally and triumphantly appointed to the position that he had so desired, of mayor of what was now truly the most beautiful village in the world.

But for Régine, little of the hubbub she could sometimes hear through the curtains made much sense to her. Her parents' agent and his gigantic wife, the housekeeper, were a ferocious pair and they refused to let anyone into the house.

They would stand, their arms folded, at the door, refusing gifts and flattery and even bribes. The young men, Régine's fascinated admirers, would be directed to the nearest shop and they would be ushered into the back room to see the paintings, which were priced higher and higher as the years went by. Or if they were just passing, or just parsimonious, they could buy small postcards of the most famous ones and would go home happy, and with an erotic glow inside that they had visited the most beautiful place and touched genius.

Failing that, they were directed to the river which

flowed slowly along, and urged to throw a few twigs in.

"This won't do, Régine," said her mother through the door, on one of her rare visits to see her daughter. "I know you're contented in there, but haven't you ever thought you would like to fall in love, or get married, or even just travel to the end of the road." M. Lapin hushed his wife: they were certain that their daughter did actually venture out at dead of night when only the ducks and the occasional fox could see her profile etched in moonlight on the road.

"Haven't you any needs, if you know what I mean?" Mme Lapin emphasised the word 'needs', but didn't elaborate. "Oh dear, it's no use. No use at all," she said, dabbing her eyes a little. But actually, it was some use, because although she had devoted herself to recreating herself on canvas, Régine did have a weakness – she did want to be loved.

She wanted to be loved for her paintings, of course – that's what she always said. They were her, after all. But in the back of her mind there was a nagging doubt. She knew the paintings were successful because people wrote to tell her – the lifelike ones from her youth as well as the wild ones with ribbons from her teenage years. Even the black ones of her own intestines from when she was 19, and now her strange abstract ones in perfumed denim. But she felt sure there was something else she needed, as if maybe somebody could adore her when they had never seen her pictures – who didn't even know about them, didn't care whether she painted or not. Was that silly? It was a ridiculous luxury, when she had devoted her life to perfecting herself, but the thought just wouldn't go away. And when her mother talked about 'needs', it enraged her because it struck a chord.

"Very well, Maman, very well," she snorted impatiently next time her mother talked like that through the trusty oak of her bedroom door. "Get me the mayor!"

"My dear, there really isn't any need for such an outburst. I was merely suggesting that you might perhaps think about marriage. Before it's too late."

"Just get him, OK?" said Régine, her heart in her mouth.

M. Le Trésourier arrived with his long black moustache and ingratiating manner, and made a great fuss about keeping his trousers straight and uncreased as he bent slowly down to speak through the keyhole.

"My dear girl. This is a great honour. Is there anything I can do for you?"

"Is there anyone there with you?" asked Régine suspiciously.

"Just my dear wife and the town clerk. And my

secretary, oh and the coach of the victorious boules team – who must by statute attend the mayor at all official…"

But Régine cut him short. "Get rid of them. I want to speak to you alone," she hissed.

There was a flurry of hands as M. Le Trésourier hussled them down the stairs and out of the house. Then, very carefully, brushing imaginary dust from where his knees would meet the carpet, and unhitching imaginary quirks in his sock suspenders, the mayor bent down again, ready to find out the will of the princess.

His face turned slowly red, and then a big smile grew to rival even his moustache.

"What was it? What was it, my dear? You did promise to tell me first?" whispered his wife as they walked home together. M. Le Trésourier made the most of his knowledge, breathed into his chest and strode tall with his new importance.

"She wishes," he said very slowly and confidingly, as if he had received secret instructions from the countess. "To get married."

Mme Trésourier gasped. "But how wonderful! What a spectacle! How delightful!"

But of course there was a snag. Before there could be any spectacle at all, any revelation of the mysterious Dauphine aux Peintures, she would need to find a husband. And since she didn't intend to leave her room to find one, that seemed an unlikely prospect.

"Well, not unlikely. Difficult, I would prefer to call it – yes I would accept that," said M. Le Trésourier judiciously. "Luckily I have an idea – or to be quite accurate – she had an idea. We will get the husband to come to her!"

Enjoying the look of confusion on his wife's face, the Mayor explained that there would be a simple test for anyone romantic or foolhardy enough to propose his hand in marriage to the Dauphine. They would have to choose which of all her paintings of herself she had ever finished came closest to portraying the real thing.

"Mais, c'est impossible!" exclaimed Claudine.

"Not impossible, my dear," said the Mayor. "Difficult, certainly, but for romance all things are possible. I don't believe the girl knows which painting is best herself, after all. So it's a question of whether a young man's choice takes her fancy somehow."

"But which young man? Can you imagine what kind of young man would submit himself to such a lottery?"

Mme Trésourier couldn't imagine, and yet the young men came, quietly some of them, others with great pomp and ceremony, down the old railway to stay at the Mayor's guest house – and would wander among the paintings staring wildly, or making pages of notes, or aimlessly and nonchalantly picking at random. They came, and they failed.

There was the merchant's son, who gazed dreamily at the river and then gave the Mayor ten bags of gold to buy some of Régine's most spectacular works. After a weekend's contemplation – interspersed with throwing the occasional stick at the ducks on the river – he chose an early version of her with hair swept back and a retroussé nose that rather excited him.

"Non!" said Régine when she heard the news.

There was the young philosopher who discussed the problem at great length with anyone who would listen. "It is a fascinating question," he told passers-by at the railway station. "First it is a matter, I think, of drawing some conclusions from the – how might I put it – totality of the work. Then applying that knowledge in such a way that it is possible to choose which one seems, in that light, the most representative work. Most intriguing. No, thank you, I'm not collecting – but thank you for the thought..."

He chose an interesting version of Régine obscured by bold blue and yellow stripes.

"Non!" said Régine when she heard. "Certainly not."

Then there was the prince himself, who arrived quietly one morning and asked for the guest house.

M. and Mme Trésourier were sent into a flurry of belated preparations when they recognised him climbing the stairs, with a shifty looking man in a bowler hat carrying his luggage up behind him. They both waited on him at breakfast, having prepared an enormous meal of braised kidneys and water melon, but he waved it away.

"Oh no, thank you so much. Just, if it wouldn't be putting you to too much trouble perhaps, a small boiled egg and a piece of dry toast."

"I can't believe you're here to marry our princess!" blurted Claudine Trésourier, in raptures before being hurriedly shushed by her husband. "That is, if I may be so bold, your highness."

"Well, you know," said the prince with suavity and graciousness. "One wants to do what one can."

But it was all no use. The prince chose a large canvas of Régine when she was a girl, with plats, in traditional pose. But when Régine was told about his choice, all she said was "Pfh!"

All day in the guest house, another young man had been getting under the feet of M. Le Trésourier as he struggled to serve the prince – and as he plucked up courage, supported by his wife, to inform him of Régine's response. Once the prince had departed in his coach, the Mayor finally exploded: "Young man, will you get out of my way!" he shouted. "I said before: I do not need another kitchen hand.

You don't what? Well, what do you want then?"

"I want to do the marriage test," he said nervously. "For La Dauphine des Peintures."

M. Le Trésourier looked at his unkempt hair and food stains on his neck. "You want what?"

"I want to do…"

"I heard, I heard. It's really quite out of the question." Really, said M. Le Trésourier to himself, what was the village coming to?

The young man slunk away, but returned the following week with a large juicy ham, earned in return for helping with the vine harvest. And he presented it to the gigantic caretakers who guarded the home of the Lapins and Régine's room. They looked a little bewildered, and perhaps just a little suspicious, but were soon clapping him on the back and offering him a drink.

The following week, he was back again, with a goatskin full of wine – which he again carried round to the home of the Lapins.

"What is that noise, mon ange?" Mme Le Trésourier asked her husband. "They seem to be carousing at Régine's home. I believe I can hear singing."

"Scandalous!" said the Mayor. "What are they thinking of? What about her work? I shall speak to them in the morning."

The following week, the young man returned with

a flagon of paté, and spent the morning drawing a beautiful sketch of one of the birds in Régine's garden, and put in a rough score for the music of one of the songs that nobody had heard for a century or more. And he wrote a note at the bottom: "Cher Dauphine de les Peintures. Today your picture feels like No. 364 (Portrait in Black with Dots and Hairband). Your friend, André." And as a special favour, he asked the guardians to put it under Régine's door – and as a special favour, the taste of paté still on their back teeth – they did.

A little later they could hear laughter inside.

"That note you gave Régine was a success," they told him the next day. "We could hear her laughing about it. Why not write another? She laughs little enough, poor girl."

So for the rest of the day, he sketched another of the birds. And scribbled their song in words, and at the bottom he sent her a message: "Cher Mademoiselle," he wrote. "I know you change from day to day like the wind. I know those who seek to pin you down like hopeless butterfly collectors, and that they can never capture you. But I feel things no prince can feel: I sense the changes as you breathe, and know that today you feel like No 621 ('Régine with Eyes and Daffodils')."

"Can it be true?" wondered Régine joyfully to herself. "Can he really feel my moods as they change, like the swaying of the poplars?" She remembered 'Eyes and Daffodils', and she did feel a little like she had when she painted No 621.

Again, the large couple who guarded her privacy heard her laughing at the note. They did not hear her pin it to the wall with all her most precious things.

The next day, the young man wrote again, and for the rest of the week, he correctly felt his way into her moods and picked the changing portraits to represent it. It was almost as if he could feel his way into her head. Régine was enchanted and, at the end of the week, she demanded to see the mayor again.

"I shall marry nobody," she informed him, "but the boy who signs himself André. Because he's done better than pick the right picture."

"What do you mean, better than picking the right picture?" said an increasingly nervous M. Le Trésourier. "That was the test! We agreed it!" The mayor became increasingly indignant as he also realised he was expected to preside in his blue, red and white sash and chain of office, and his tricorn had with plume, at the wedding of their princess with a boy who he suspected had aspired to little more than washing bottles.

"My dear Régine," he said, masking his rage with increasing difficulty. "I simply cannot allow you to..."

"Cannot? I can't believe you said that, M. Le Trésourier. There is no cannot. That young man hit a moving target. Please tell André to talk to me."

And so it was that a nervous young man, dressed in the best-ironed clothes he had ever worn, walked up the bedroom stairs that afternoon. Behind him strode and red-faced M. Le Trésourier, who knocked on the door and witnessed for the first time in two decades the door prised open before his very eyes, dust falling from the doorframe, a few balls of ancient fluff bursting out from underneath, and one dead moth falling briefly onto the Mayor's spotless suit.

Then there she was, a little pale perhaps, but her cheeks glowing and her paint-bespattered smock – and the detritus of 20 years of relentless creativity – a testament to what she had made of herself. The couple stood staring happily at each other, then the boy put out both hands and grasped hers and somehow their smiles were infectious. Soon M. and Mme Le Trésourier were smiling too, and the large couple who looked after her too, and M. and Mme Lapin, her parents, were smiling and a smile seemed to creep across the village, bending the old bridge just a little, stiffening the railway lines, and sending flocks of Régine's beloved birds joyfully into the air.

"But you can't give up painting!" said a shocked M. Le Trésourier to her later – the second time that day he had felt his heart palpitating during an uncomfortable interview with the princess. "What about us? What would happen to the village?"

"But it's time to change, Monsieur. Or rather it's time not to change," she said. "It's time to live in the world like a human being."

Desperately, he sent her parents to remonstrate, but Régine was adamant."

"You see, I have hidden all these years behind my pictures," she told them. "Now I want to be myself. I don't want to be a work of art any more. I want to be real."

"Oh Régine, that is so childish," said her mother. "How can you be yourself? We all need a little help to face the world."

But as always, Régine got her own way. She stared a long time at herself in the mirror, locked the door of her bedroom – her home for so long – behind her and dressed the following week finally in white, with just a feather in her hair. And she walked down the aisle on the arm of her father, towards a waiting M. Le Trésourier and a patient André smiling back at her.

Later he carried her laughing over the threshold. Then she went back upstairs and came back down in an ordinary skirt of sackcloth and a rug. "This is me," she said, leaping lightly into the room. He hugged her close to him, and outside the birds sang with redoubled force.

She wore the same thing the next day, as they

walked arm in arm down the river. And again the day after as they wandered into the forest. And the day after that, and the week after that, and the month after that. At last I can be myself, she told herself.

Régine rejoiced at her stillness, her sense of permanence, and her feeling of herself unmediated through pictures. She felt like the real thing for the first time in her life. But she couldn't help noticing a kind of far away look in her husband's eyes.

She thought little about it until one morning she came down early, jauntily as usual, fed the songbirds and then saw a single sheet of notepaper on the table waiting for her.

"Dear Régine," she read.

"This note is to say that, though it breaks my heart to do so, I must leave. I love you from my head to my toes, and yet I find I am living with someone I don't know. I felt my way into your changeability for that wonderful week because you were a mystery, and now I find myself confronted every day by your unchangability, and I fear for myself. I waft this way and that like the poplars, but you stay still like a strange stone. I am the changing sea that breaks on your rock. I can hardly bear to hurt you, and yet I have changed and must go. May God be with you."

Régine screwed up the paper, walked slowly upstairs, unlocked her bedroom door, waved to the birds, squeezed out a tube of yellow oil onto her palette and began to paint. And as she did so, the great wave of sadness that hit her suddenly began to disappear, and she found herself whistling the songs of the birds outside and painted like she had never painted before – and not just herself, but the world outside.

So the mayor was happy again that the famous daughter of the village had returned and was turning herself back into a work of art.

The large couple came home and they were happy. Even M. and Mme Lapin were happy that their daughter was home and secure.

Only André, the changing boy, sat thousands of miles away dreaming of his weeks with the great Princess of the Pictures – whose creations he saw reproduced wherever he went – and longing to see her just once more. But as she really was.

Basingstoke

"And clean the rugs while you're about it. You ragamuffin.

"Can you believe it," said the loud man in a scarlet coat as his voice echoed down the corridors. "I just found the gipsy boy sitting back trying to read the newspaper!"

Poor Basingstoke. His life had never been easy, as far as he could remember – and he couldn't remember very far – but the last fortnight had been almost impossible. And he could never have read the newspaper even if he tried, as his tormentors knew very well.

Ever since Sir Richard became ill, and the house had echoed to the pounding of nurses' feet, and the clanging of doorbells as doctors and half-forgotten relatives had arrived at the front door.

Some of the least pleasant relatives had actually stayed, leaving their boots on the doorstep. It was an old affectation of the ancient Broadbent family, who had ruled this village and its surroundings since the

Conquest, that guests should leave their boots behind before entering the house.

When they noticed him at all, the relatives treated him like a plantation slave. Do this. Do that. Carry this. Sweep this staircase. Clean up that disgusting mess on the pantry flagstones.

His dark-skinned presence in the house had unnerved the relatives at first. They had been talking loudly, in braying voices: then they caught sight of him, and stopped suddenly, staring disconcertedly.

The men, in heavy red coats, had carried on staring. It was left to the more articulate women to put into words exactly the question they wanted to ask.

"What is your name, child?"

"He's no child. Look at those feet."

"I said, what is your name?"

"Basingstoke," said Basingstoke. The articulate women giggled with surprise. But they looked under his long dark eyebrows and picked up the fear in his eyes, and it bored them.

Sometimes they would press the point that he should speak to then with more respect. "Basingstoke *ma'am*," they would say determinedly. "Heavens, I sound like the inspector at a railway station!"

Usually they drifted away in a cloud of white lace and scent, and you could hear their peels of laughter down the cold passages.

"Oh well," said the men. "Clean my boots. I've had to leave them on the doorstep. Ridiculous idea, but we must humour Sir Richard mustn't we," he exchanged a lascivious glance with his cousins.

Basingstoke could hear their voices braying around the house. "Why ARE we expected to leave our boots by the door?"

"You remember, it's the bally old family curse. An outsider with boots will inherit the estate. So we never let boots into the house."

"Why? I know the best families have curses. But what a boring one! Why couldn't it be about bloodcurdling screams or black birds on the battlements like everybody else's?"

"You know perfectly well. It was old Sir Roderick's seduction of a girl from the village. Drowned herself in the fishpond. Centuries ago. Far too late for the curse now, I would have thought."

It was 300 years if it was a day, but for most of the village people, the curse was all they knew of the estate – except for the kindness of Sir Richard who unfortunately seemed to get madder and madder. But then he was a bachelor, wasn't he.

Like the estate, the house was ancient and freezing cold, even in the spring. Outside the blossom was on the trees in the orchard. There was an extra spring in the steps of the cattle as they passed along the road. Birds twittered optimistically. Inside the dour portraits of Sir Richard's ancestors looked down as coldly as ever – uptight women with pendulous jewels and shining breasts, men in ruffs, cavaliers filling the canvass with a kind of dead panache.

But it was easy for Basingstoke to keep warm: there was so much to do every day. The silver had to be cleaned. Sir Richard's great black boots – which lived in the porch – had to have the mud scraped from them. The candles had to be cut, and the great oak table in the hall had to be polished. Then there were stables to be seen to, wood to be cut, fires to be cleaned out and then lit again.

And sometimes, late in the evening, Sir Richard used to call to him as he drank his last port of the night, a little too close to the fire, with its pictures and mementoes of long-forgotten hunting expeditions, and its memories of drunken huntsmen throwing their glasses into the flames.

Then Basingstoke would sit by the fire and Sir Richard would regale him the country tales collected in a long rural bachelor's life. Of foxes killed, of women deflowered, of operas and balls long ago.

And the dust above the fireplace absorbed it all and lay heavy with the weight of centuries.

But not now. For the past month, Sir Richard's final decline had been gathering momentum. He had taken to his bed. His breathing had become rasping. The doctors had bled him painfully, and still he insisted on his final pint of port before turning in for the night.

As soon as it became widely known that Sir Richard might not recover, the visits of the doctor – and the wizened old family lawyer – were followed by whole coaches of new relatives, hoping to be remembered in the will.

Once every day or so, Sir Richard continued to call for Basingstoke. And, avoiding the disapproving stares of the visiting relatives, he crept upstairs, past the empty suit of armour and the tattered banner, black with age, into the bedroom.

And there was Sir Richard, looking shrivelled in the enormous bed, with the white porcelain jug on the wooden chest, and the twigs in the park outside the lozenged window.

As he crept away again, Basingstoke could hear snippets of the relatives' remarks.

"Who is the boy anyway?"

"Where does he come from?"

"...found him alone outside some town in Hampshire, I believe..."

"...brought him home...."

Basingstoke felt out of place. He had been in the house eight years, since he had been abandoned by his wandering family – presumably to die of hunger or exposure in the lonely Hampshire fields.

Sir Richard had seen him through the driving rain, as his coachman had forced the pace to return before midnight. He had questioned him, brought him home and there he had remained. He feared for the future when Sir Richard died.

It wasn't just that Sir Richard's death would probably propel him back into the world outside. There was the family curse to worry about too. Basingstoke dreaded the arrival of one of the relatives, but he dreaded the complete stranger in boots even more.

Basingstoke only knew about this because, in the old days, Sir Richard would joke about it and even recount the strange verse:

"Your family will rue this day:
A foreigner will have his way.
Because you have too little merit,
The man in boots will you inherit."

Recently, Sir Richard had found the curse far less amusing. Basingstoke could only remember him mentioning it once in the last five years – and he did so with a chuckle. "I believe I've scotched that old witch," he said before a giant swig of port made him cough and splutter.

Basingstoke missed the homely chuckle so much

that he could hardly bear it. He hadn't heard it for months, and the laughs of the relatives who had come to stay were deeply unpleasant. There was one cousin with a nasal twang which was audible inside the house while Basingstoke was digging up vegetables, beyond what remained of the formal garden. And one woman laughed like baying hounds. He came to dread her sense of humour.

They stopped laughing – even stopped talking – whenever he came into the room, usually with a brush or a coal scuttle. But the house was ancient and echoing, and if he found himself down in the cellars, assisting with the task of slaking the thirst of the cousins, he could sometimes hear the occasional sentence.

"The old boy can't have long," said one of the relatives.

"I hope not," said the nasal cousin with a neigh. "I have to be back in town within the fortnight. And there's the race meet. I don't intend to miss that, whatever the old man puts in his will."

Then the clanging of the doorbell brought Basingstoke back up from the dusty cellar, carrying a grey and ageing bottle of port, hurrying to answer the door.

It was the doctor, and he spent some minutes struggling with his boots, the powder from his wig swirling around him like a cloud of dust. As he made his way up to Sir Richard's room, the relatives bustled up the stairs after him, pushing each other out of the way.

"Get those leeches out of here," said Sir Richard in a weak voice, as two of the cousins tried to squeeze through the door simultaneously.

"Oh come, Uncle! We are concerned for your health! Let us in," they said together, knocking over a hat stand.

"Out! You heard what Uncle Richard said!" said a pompous relative, with the foresight to install himself a few minutes before. "Can I get you anything, Uncle? Some water perhaps? Some snuff?"

"Oh yes, it's your bedroom already, is it," said the sarcastic relative with the laugh like a pack of hounds – and only just quiet enough to prevent Sir Richard hearing.

"OUT!" said the doctor. "Out! I need to be able to consult with my patient!"

Slowly and complainingly the relatives moved out of the room. "Who does he think he is?" said one, as they grumbled their way downstairs. "If he bleeds him any more we'll be left with a husk," said another. "I wouldn't let him lose on my horse."

"You'd spend more curing your horse than you would your own wife."

"Certainly I would. The horse is worth far more.

And I can hardly ride the wife to hounds, can I?" He roared with laughter.

Basingstoke shuffled between laying the fires and the pantry, trying to appear inconspicuous.

"Gipsy!" called one of the relatives, slowly descending the staircase. "I have some work for you to do."

"Oh and so do I," piped up one of the ladies from the next room. And soon Basingstoke was working through a heavy pile of buckles which needed to be shining and was sewing up a hole on a pair of thick leggings.

"And mind you get it done by this evening. I need those later," she said as her small feet echoed down the corridor.

It was, after all, a house of many echoes. But the echo after the doctor's visit, like a rush of wind down the passages, ruffling the bed-hangings and blowing the dust off the ancient words on the walls, was not good for Sir Richard.

He seemed to be fading fast. Soon he could protest no more, and his bedroom filled with cackling relatives, talking about racing in loud voices and pacing backwards and forwards in the room.

At dawn the next morning, the doctor left the house, wrapping his cloak around him as he trudged down the drive to his horse. Basingstoke felt sick as he paced backwards and forwards down the hall listening for news.

The relatives were mostly still asleep after a heavy session with the contents of Sir Richard's cellar the previous night. One of the empty bottles lay forgotten beside the remains of the fire. A cold light filled the house. He felt his hopes struggling against the implacable morning light.

At long last there was a click of the handle of Sir Richard's door, and a nurse emerged, looking drained. Sir Richard had given up the struggle. Basingstoke wept.

The relatives emerged through the morning, undaunted by the news, and the noise of their hearty breakfast filtered around the house. But as his body lay washed and laid out upstairs, Sir Richard's solicitor arrived at the front door.

Basingstoke pulled the great oak beam open and found the wizened lawyer laying his boots with precision on the front doorstep, their toes pointing uniformly up the hill to the village.

He nodded and came into the house, followed by a mighty draft from the estate which had been waiting patiently like a cat to get into the house. The solicitor rubbed his spectacles as he bustled in, a large folder under his arm with little pieces of red ribbon hanging down from it.

He was clearly expected, and was ushered into the main room, where Basingstoke had been told to lay and light the fire.

While the lawyer sat himself down and began to sort through his papers, Basingstoke carried on arranging the wetter logs nearer to the flames. And the relatives began to drift in with an air of expectancy. Some of them were talking loudly about foxes or unusual routes between nearby villages and pubs. Some had been drinking already.

"Well you take the main turnpike road until the Duke's Head, then you turn off onto a muddy track for about half a mile..."

"Let's hope the old boy's had a bit of sense," muttered the relative with the laugh. "I've been waiting for this will to be read for weeks now."

The room grew quiet as they assembled. The wizened solicitor fussed with the papers.

"And now...um... thank you for assembling at such short notice," he said, peering over his spectacles. "I have the will here, and if we are all ready, I shall dispense with the preliminaries and read it out."

Still busy with the fire, Basingstoke was listening with his heart in his mouth. He knew the relatives were looking at him imperiously, expecting him to leave, but he wanted to know which of them would be master of his fate.

"I Richard Broadbent, being of sound mind...." read the solicitor haltingly.

"Out!" said one of the relatives sharply. "Get the gipsy boy out of here."

Basingstoke hurried to collect his small dustpan and brush and practically fell out of the fireplace in his effort to leave quickly.

But as he reached the door, the solicitor stopped him. "Oh er, I think, if you wouldn't mind, you should stay, young man. I believe you are mentioned in the will. Perhaps I could...er...continue...?"

"The gipsy! In the will! Pshhh. The poor old man must have been absolutely gaga," said one of the women relatives to her next door neighbour audibly. Everyone was embarrassed as Basingstoke crept back in, carrying his dustpan with him.

But the will took less than a minute to read. Basingstoke understood almost nothing, but did hear his name mentioned at the end. There was a sharp intake of breath around the room. Then stunned silence.

"You see, my boy, Sir Richard has... er... left the house and the estate to *you*," said the solicitor to him.

More silence.

"I don't believe it," said another relative in a strangled voice. "There must be some mistake."

"I assure you there is not. I witnessed this will myself only a few months ago," said the solicitor. Another relative walked quickly from the room, slamming the door. They heard him scrunching on the gravel outside as he marched to the stables.

Basingstoke was astonished and sweating with embarrassment until he could stand it no longer. He slipped off his chair and made for the door as quickly as he could.

The relatives, their faces in a rainbow of colours from peuce to bright red, heard his working boots echoing on the flagstones down the corridor outside.

Lost

Once there was a kingdom, not far from here, where the corn always grew as high as the night owls and the badgers spent the dark hours weaving delicate clothes of starlight.

It was a happy kingdom, where the country people sang in the daylight and the city people sang at night. The farmers were happy, the king was happy and his family, musicians, knights, magicians and servants were happy, too. Only small problems ever furrowed their brows, but they would think deeply and the answers would pop almost unbidden into their heads.

But despite all this wisdom and happiness, they lived the shortest lives. By the time they were 20, they were almost middle-aged. By the time they were 30, they were old. The generations passed by quickly and smilingly into the dust. But they knew no different and filled the years they had with joy and music and hunting.

Only one person in the whole kingdom had a problem which seemed beyond resolution, and he hugged it to himself, searching for an answer. That was the prince, the eldest son and heir to the throne. He lived in great finery, with tapestries of exotic beasts hanging from the walls of his room, and daily breakfasts of quails' eggs and baths of the best warm wine.

Yet one small flaw in his character kept him awake night after night. He kept losing things. They were insignificant things at first. He lost the key to the great trunk where he kept his most beautiful robes. Though his servants scoured the palace from top to bottom on his behalf, there was absolutely no sign of it and the trunk had to be forced open with a metal bar.

He lost his favourite dagger, with pearls and rubies on the hilt and a kiss from the most beautiful princess in the world planted firmly on the blade. He had it with him only the night before. It was extraordinary how his things just disappeared.

He even lost his favourite horse. He just stopped for a nap by the road during a long ride back from the outlying provinces, and when he had woken up, it was gone. Though he called its name until his throat was sore, though he led a hundred followers calling through the forest, all they ever found was a silver horseshoe and some tell-tale prints in the mud. It was not the most serious problem in the world, but it kept the prince worrying into the small hours. It was all very well losing things when he was just a prince. He had access to untold wealth, so there was no difficulty replacing trunks, daggers and horses. But what about when he was king – which could only be soon now that his father was well into his 30s? He could hardly go around losing things then. He might lose a province or two if he was careless. Worse, he might lose a battle. What could he do?

On his 15th birthday – when the young people of that kingdom came of age – the presents and letters flooded into the palace from cities of which he had never even heard. There were tapestries woven by badgers. There were ceremonial quails and translucent daggers, their blades kissed by the most fertile women. There were pictures and goblets and princesses and advice. And at the end of the day of celebration and feasting, he was preparing himself for bed, and there was a knock at the door.

It was his old nurse and he threw his arms around her neck. She told him that, now he was 15, it was time for her to leave the palace and go back to her family in one of the most distant provinces, where the trees grew directly upwards and it was always night. 'But before I leave I have a special present for you, which I have kept secret all these years, and which I am sure was made to solve your difficulties,' she said.

She took him in slippers and on tiptoe through

the quiet back corridors of the sleeping palace, to a door the prince had never seen before. It had a tapestry in front of it which hid it from view and great iron rivets to hold it in place.

'What is in this room?' said the prince, intrigued by the secret.

'I will show you,' said his nurse, knocking three times on the topmost rivet and turning the handle. Inside was a gigantic window, and through it in the fading light, the prince could still make out the shapes of trees, castles and houses and in the distance, glinting in the new moon, the sails of great ships waiting in the harbour.

'But this is not the view from my palace. Where am I looking?' he asked.

'That is the kingdom of the lost,' said the nurse, with a stern authority he had never heard from her before. 'Everything anybody has ever lost is there. So this is my gift to you, my beautiful boy,' she said. 'If you have lost something you value, come secretly to this room, open the window and call to it across the roofs and you will see it coming to you. Only be very careful. You must use this gift sparingly and only for unimportant things. Sometimes what we lose must be lost, and you must know when this is. If it is an important thing, you must leave it in its proper place.'

'I do not understand you,' said the prince, his

initial delight turning to irritation. 'If they are not important, why should I want them back?'

The nurse guffawed. 'Come now! Have I not seen you calling and cursing about unimportant things like keys and daggers and horses? Here – open the window and call your missing horse and see what happens.'

So the prince opened the window, felt the night breeze on his face and saw the people moving slowing around the town below. Drawing a deep breath, he shouted 'Galahad!'

There was a flutter of wings as the crows nesting on the palace roof took flight, and a moment's silence through the city of the lost below. Then unmistakably, he could hear the clip-clop of a horse making its way down the road to the palace, and there was his missing Galahad, whinnying to itself outside the gates.

'I can hardly believe it! What an extraordinary gift! It is by far the greatest gift I have ever been given!'

'Yes, my child, but do not whatever you do forget my warning ...'

But the prince was already through the door with the rivets and making for the palace gates to welcome his horse. By the time he came back, the door with the rivets was firmly shut and his old nurse was gone, but in the years that followed, he heeded her advice.

He was careful to use the magical room and its extraordinary window only rarely. He used it to find a ring with a topaz from the furthest East which he had lost somewhere in the palace gardens, but when he lost some books in the town, he shrugged his shoulders. He used it to recover a bag of gold belonging to one of his sisters, which he lost on the way to the market, but when he lost his favourite necktie he just let it go – and bought another one twice as good.

When the most beautiful princess in the whole world rejected his offer of marriage and slipped through his fingers and rode off to her own distant province beyond the mountains, he longed for her. He spent almost a week without sleep wondering whether to tiptoe to the room and call to her and hear her trotting back to him. But he knew it was just too important – and anyway, maybe she would come back of her own accord. He congratulated himself on his strength of will and on keeping his nurse's condition.

Then one day his father, the old king, died at the grand old age of 38. The whole city wore black for a month, and a thousand lambs were slaughtered for the funeral feast. The prince escaped to his quarters, and barred the door – until his mother, his sisters and the king's council came hammering on it, demanding that he should come out.

The prince knew he must. Sheepishly, he unbarred the door and was led away to his ritual washing, his ritual dressing and his coronation. As they walked slowly down the main corridor, the King's Council badgered him with questions. 'I know this is a difficult time for you, Sire. But it is most important that we take a decision on the south east frontier where the tribes are behaving in a most disturbing way.'

'I wonder if you might quickly turn your attention to the case of Tom the Cobbler whose plea for clemency must be decided by midnight tonight ...'

'We have the menus for the Coronation Banquet here for you, Sire. I wonder, though, if we should be seating the Earl of the North Desert quite so close to the Bishop of the Long Forgotten Isles. I fear that would be asking for trouble ...'

The prince nodded nervously and shook his head, and his courtiers and advisers seemed to be satisfied and scuttled away to carry out what they clearly believed were his instructions. But inside, his stomach was turning to quicksand. He missed his father enormously for his comforting words, his thoughtful advice, and he simply could not understand the questions he was being asked. He had never even heard of the South East Frontier. They could have seated Tom the Cobbler next to the

Earl of the North Desert for all he cared.

Yet he had to care. He would make some disastrous mistake and the bishop would raise an army and the kingdom would be ruined. Or worse. Any number of appalling possibilities passed through his mind. He simply could not do it. What a time to lose his father! It was important, but it really was vital for the kingdom that his father should be found. Could the magic room and the magic window put right such fundamental losses?

It was too important, probably, for his nurse's warnings – but it simply had to be tried. The future of the kingdom depended on it. So it was that, on the night before his coronation, he tiptoes in his stockings down the corridors and up the spiral stairs, knocked three times on the rivets and slipped into the room. He unclasped the window and felt the warm grassy air of the summer night.

Then with all his might, he called for his father. The word echoed over the rooftops. He froze to hear if anyone in the household had been disturbed. Then unmistakably, he could hear footsteps approaching the drawbridge below, and the clink of his father's armour and the sound of his familiar cough, then his voice, then he could almost feel him pounding on the great oak doors to the palace.

His heart in his mouth, the prince dashed downstairs, not pausing to refasten the door, and ordering the guards to open the gates – and flung his arms around his father's neck. But his father seemed unmoved by the meeting. In fact, he seemed to be in a terrible rage.

When the palace awoke the next morning and, to their astonishment and fear, found the old king as healthy as ever and sitting on the throne, the plans for the coronation were quietly abandoned amid much whispering. So life returned to normal. Nobody mentioned to the old king that they had thought him dead. The prince returned to his lessons. The coronation robes and crown jewels were put silently away – only now life seemed strangely different.

The prince found that he now lost nothing at all. Many of the things he had thought lost now turned up in their proper place, including the missing princess – which was inconvenient because he was now admiring a different one. Even the things he discarded were back the next morning. Old clothes, old dishcloths, old handkerchiefs appeared back on the shelf. Within a week or so, his shelves and cupboards were growing under the weight.

Worse, his mind seemed to be seizing up – not because he kept forgetting things as usual, but because he forgot nothing. His memory was cluttering up with the most irrelevant facts and overheard conversations – and embarrassing moments that he desperately wanted to forget all hammered away inside his head.

He soon noticed that something similar was happening to everyone in the palace. Nothing could be discarded. The slops and rubbish put out each night were back the next morning. Soon they cramped the kitchen and passageways and a sour human smell wafted down the corridors. Everyone seemed furious all the time. As the weeks went by, he could also hear them complaining about the king. 'He's stale,' they said. 'We need something new. Fresh ideas. Youth. He's a great man, of course, but he's stuck in the past. The prince should have his turn.'

But they were all stuck mysteriously in the past, though nobody spoke of it. And the prince could see as well that, down in the city, the piles of rubbish and the angry constipated faces showed that the problem had spread there, too. Nothing could be lost and life was grinding to a halt. The weather stopped. The seasons stopped. Dead patriarchs dropped back for unexpected visits. Colds stayed put. Moods stayed put. Nobody changed their minds. Nobody changed at all – yet because they did not change, they also changed all too much.

In desperation, the prince escaped to the magic room, knocked on the rivets, opened the window – only to find that, this time, the view was the old familiar one of his own palace and his own city below. He ordered the door bricked up, ordered his horse and set off for the far province where it was always night.

Days later, he knew he had reached it because of the chilly wind and the dawn that did not arrive. Asking at every house he came too, he was finally directed to a small cottage with a tartan door and there was his old nurse, just as she always had been. He flung himself on his knees in front of her, sobbing and begging her to forgive his stupidity and rescue the kingdom.

'Tsk tsk,' she said. 'I blame myself. The temptation was just too much. But I hope this has been a lesson to you. There are some things you just have to lose. That is all there is to it.'

Then she went out into the back garden, and called to the badgers and night owls in a strange language the prince had never heard before. Then the wind got up and swirled through the hedges in the dark, buffeting them and making them twist. There was a flash of light, a bang and a strange noise, like cracking ice, a trickle of water and then a gushing torrent.

'Well, that is that,' said the nurse. 'You must now go home.'

As he approached his own city, he could see people sweeping their front doorsteps, and the streets clean and sparkling in the morning sunlight. The piles of stinking rubbish had completely gone. 'We really must arrange your coronation,' said his chamberlain back in the palace, as if in mid-conversation.

As the years of his reign went by, and he rapidly grew in age and wisdom, he still lost his socks, his money, his ornamental badgers and occasionally his way. So he was sometimes tempted to look for the little room with the enormous window where he could find the things he lost. But every time he searched the strange corridor, feeling his way along the brickwork for the door, he simply could not find it.

Loch Nowhere

My name is Jeremy Guest and I am writing this deposition in the hope that somehow it will be able to reach my family – though, frankly, I find it hard to believe such a feat will be possible. For reasons you will perhaps understand when you have read it.

It contains a number of events that I would hardly have believed myself had they not happened to me, and even now I doubt myself somewhat. They begin with a barely believable encounter in Scotland, where I happened to be working at the time, attempting to finish a book in the seclusion.

I was staying, you must understand, on the shores of Loch Nevis on the west Highland coast, some way from civilisation. I arrived by boat. In fact, I believe there was then no road there from Mallaig, the nearest town. It was a beautiful spot and I had travelled there alone to finish the book that was behind schedule, tentatively entitled *Twenty-First Century Public Services*. Perhaps its main disadvantage was that it was somewhat damp. Rivers and rivulets poured down the rocks from the hills all around. Every day, even in July and August, it seemed to rain at some point in the day and one was constantly drying one's shoes and clothes next to the fire.

It was a particularly virulent shower that caught me, some way from the house, that afternoon, without an anorak and I struggled to find some shelter. By luck – at least, it seemed so at the time – I was next to a small wooden bridge that crossed one of the powerful waterfalls that speed down into the loch from above. I peered hopefully beneath the bridge, because I would otherwise have been drenched.

My heart leaped a little as I saw a small ledge under there by the fast running water and swung myself under quickly. What did surprise me, however, was that the ledge turned out to be considerably larger than I had imagined. Indeed, it opened out into the darkness and gloom along the side of the stream.

It was immediately clear that I was not alone.

A cheery voice came out of the darkness. It sounded Scottish.

"Hello, welcome my dear sir! I insinuate that you got caught too, did you not?"

"I certainly did," I said. "I didn't see you ahead of me on the path."

"Ah, well," said my companion. "I think I've been

here through many of the storms recently."

These had certainly been numerous, so this sentence did not at the time strike me as odd. Though clearly it did later.

"Here!" he said. "I have a couple of spare biscuits if you'd like to share them."

"That's extremely good of you," I said, accepting the proffered gift, though had still not been able to make out the giver with my own eyes.

It seemed strangely rustic, I had to say. "Unusual taste. Sort of health food, I suppose?"

"Ye coulda saye tha'," said my new friend, laughing uproariously. I could hear the rain beating down on the bridge above us. I could hear his Scottish accent too.

It was that this point that my eyes began to get used to our gloomy hiding place, and I have to say I was surprised again. My new friend, it was becoming clear, was some variety of very small person. Perhaps, I suppose, about three feet high, but in proportion like a man. I had believed him to be sitting rather further away. In reality, he was quite close.

I stared, but he didn't appear to notice.

"What is your name, my friend?" he said. "I have other things we might add to the feast before the storm clears, if you should like that?"

"My name?" I said, rather flustered. "Oh, um,

Jeremy. I usually try to avoid health food if I can," I said, aware suddenly that this made me sound like a prig. Then, to my surprise, he pulled out – though I could not see where from – half a packet of Jaffa Cakes. This time, it was my turn to laugh.

"Good lord, you're a surprise a minute," I said, inexplicably relieved. "I should ask your name, since you know mine."

"My name is Idric of the Loch," he said. "What did you expect? Rumplestiltskin?"

"Why would I expect that?" I said, a little confused. "Here, I mustn't eat all your Jaffa Cakes."

I could see now that he was dressed in a kind of long leather coat which appeared in the darkness to be the same colour as he was, a sort of brown, leathery hue. I could not make him out or allocate him to any kind of category.

"Well, should you want to get home once more, you will need to find me again. Is that not so? And now, I see the rain has lifted and I will leave you. Farewell, Jeremy. I hope to see you again."

I watched him jump out of our hiding place with astonishment, since he was considerably more sprightly than I had expected. I realised I had imagined myself conversing with an old man.

For a moment I was too stunned to move, but realised – as I tried to categorise the experience I had just encountered – that he had been correct about the weather. I lay back in my mud cave and I suppose I must have dozed off, because it was clearly much later when I peered out again. The sun was lower in the sky and the temperature was considerably warmer.

I am not a credulous man but I realised, even then, by the state of my clothes, that I had undergone some kind of supernatural experience. The wool garments I had been wearing had rotted in the damp, though luckily most of my clothes were nylon and had survived the trauma of being underground. I had heard stories about fairies of course – who hasn't? – but of course I never actually believed them in the here and now. Suddenly, of course, I was not so sure.

I clambered out, brushed myself down, noticing with irritation and embarrassment all the mudstains on my underclothes. It really looked as though I had slept there for decades, I joked to myself – little did I know. Then I drew myself up and looked around, absolutely astonished.

The first thing that caught my eye was a huge orange hood next to my bridge. It said 'Hydro energy unit provided by Knoydart Utilities Ltd'. It was as I wondered how I could have missed such a garish installation that I looked further and then I began to be a little scared, I confess.

How had I failed to realise there were so many human habitations along the side of the loch? How had I missed all this activity on the shore – all these boats which were criss-crossing the water, some sailing and some hovering a little over the surface, powered by what I could only describe as a gentle hum as they glided by? Had I slept through the start of some kind of regatta?

I looked up and down the mountainside and realised that every little burn and waterfall had its own yellow or orange canopy. It was then that I understood that I must be having some kind of hallucination. When a dream comes to you complete, in the sense that it appears completely real and you have to give up trying to pinch yourself awake, I wondered whether perhaps my whole holiday had been the hallucination. When had it begun, after all?

I began to be really frightened. Gathering what I could of my rotten clothes, I walked as fast as I could back to the house I had been staying in. As I walked past a range of the homes built along the foothills of the slopes, and becoming increasingly astonished and frightened as I did so, I realised that the sea was also five or six feet higher than I remembered and, by the time I reached the path that should have taken me down to the beach where my lodging was, I knew the truth before I got there. There was the sea. Beyond it and below it, presumably, was my house. And my book, of course.

My illusion – or so I still imagined it – was that I

had fallen asleep and dreamed my way forward by some decades, maybe even a century. I have written quite widely about the future and, even if the whole thing emanated from my imagination, I was fascinated by it. I decided to search out someone I could talk to about it.

There was a makeshift pier nearby and I saw a couple walking along it and went down to meet them. They were helpful, and seemed oddly dressed – whoever thought of wearing a ruff and tights?

"I have been away some time. I've been in America," I told them. "Do you, by any chance, have a local historian I could converse with?"

"Man, I know just the guy you want!" he said. "You want Hamish."

"That is excellent. You could possibly direct me and introduce me, I would be eternally grateful."

"Totally," said the man.

Some minutes later, we stood together, knocking at a door. "Hello!" shouted my friend. "I have a visitor for you: this is my uncle, Hamish McAbdul - this is Msr ... um... ?" He gave me a questioning look.

"Guest," I said. I was about to receive my next shock.

"Msr Guest!" he said, waving an arm without getting up. "Come in, come in! Forgive me – my legs have long since stopped operating. You are no relation, I suppose to Jeremy Guest, famous once in these parts?"

"Relation! I *am* him!" I said, with some joy and relief.

To my surprise, my new friend laughed and repeated his invitation to come in, waving his nephew goodbye.

"Strange coincidence that, because, as you may know, there was a time a century ago when someone called the same name as you went missing in peculiar circumstances. That Msr Guest has not been seen since, I fear. In fact, do you see that white column sticking out of the sea about fifty yards from here? No, not that way – near that dhow that's just going by. See it? That was the old Jeremy Guest Memorial set up by his family back in 2021. That's how I know his name. It is still visible sometimes at low tide and so it's familiar to me. I say, whatever is the matter? Come and sit down, human…"

A sense of horror had gripped me as he told me this. My dream – if that is what it was - was fast becoming a nightmare. A whole range of possibilities swam inside my head, each one less pleasant than the last. All I could do, I felt, was to tell the truth as I saw it.

"The thing is" – I could barely speak – "you won't believe this, I fear, but I think it was me. It *was* me. I don't know how, or what kind of dream we are in, but I may have disappeared into this nightmare or this future tense. Please tell me: what year is it?

"The year? It is 2119, human. Come and talk to me, you interest me strangely. As they used to say."

I told him my story, which – as I expected – he didn't really believe, and he told me his. How the seas had risen and the weather had got warmer and how he had come here as a boy, the grandson of refugees from Syria, before the huge rush of population northwards with the changing climate.

"So we survived the great warming, then? I suppose we must have done."

"We survived by taking action. Humanity, I mean. So far, and the planet is still getting hotter, or so I understand, but not nearly so fast. We have also had to survive civil war too but, again, we managed to arrest those on both sides who were pursuing it."

"Civil war? How so?"

"Ah well," said Hamish dismissively. "That is all some time ago now. Back in the 2020s and 40s. It followed the break-up of the UK. It must have been a strange time, though I wasn't there, of course. It led in the end to the imprisonment for sedition of many leading figures who had encouraged armed rebellion to protect the old United Kingdom. These turned out to be the same ones often who had organised the exit of Britain from the old European Union and, before that, had worked hard to prevent any of the necessary changes to prevent us all being overwhelmed by new weather."

"Of course! Brexit! What happened?"

"You don't know? Well, it all turned out to be rather unimportant because the European Union didn't survive long in that state anyway. But by then the damage had been done to our own union. The Scots left. So did Northern Ireland, and so the civil wars began. It was a traumatic period around the time I was born. You can't break up old empires without these kind of emotions emerging."

"How was it resolved? The civil wars, I mean?"

"Well, as you may know – where did you say you were from again? - Europe is now fifty or sixty nations, all independent and yet connected, just as we are here. Scotland is one of the biggest. But we all live under the auspices of the FBI..."

"The FBI?" I said. "The Federal Bureau of In..."

"No no no – the Federation of the British Isles. We're still nominally a monarchy. King George X still reigns. In a sense, anyway."

"So help me out here...," a little confused. "Which is the nation? Scotland, England or this FBI?"

"All and none!" said Hamish, laughing. "All and none! It is a pattern that most other European nations have copied. As you must know," he said, momentarily forgetting my story, as well he might. "Now can I get you a dram?"

We talked on. Outside, the sun went down, the

darkness fell and the only sound that wafted through the windows of my new friend was occasional laughter, the lapping waters and the hum of hydropower.

He told me how battery power had changed the world. How everything, every home, every building, every metre of road, every brick and every window generated energy; how was there was no shortage of energy any more. How this allowed small communities, like the one he lived in, to fend for themselves – and small nations too – in a way that only the big ones had been able to before.

He told me how the functions of energy and money have begun to merge into *monergy*, and how this led to a proliferation – not just of communities – but also of currencies. His neighbours used a whole variety of these for different aspects of their lives. He explained how this had allowed the devolution of power far lower than before and how, generally, this made people more peaceable. Less cross.

"And every month, from the Scottish government, we all get paid enough to get by on – okay in their own Scottish money, which I wouldn't choose myself. It is controversial again now..."

"How so?" I asked.

"There are those who believe basic income prevents us from being more outward looking – it means we have to protect our shores from refugees because we can't afford for them to come. And on the other side, there are those who want us to go back to the good old 20th century, with big armies, massed consumers, huge growth, great wealth. I need hardly say that I am not one of them..."

We talked on, about how change happens in unexpected ways, sometimes despite its defeat, and how it leads on to more change and more demands. It was, I believed, one of the best conversations I have ever had in my life and, by the end of it, my head was absolutely spinning with concepts, some familiar, some completely unfamiliar.

It was almost as if humanity had managed to take the one path possible for survival and had stuck to it. And, in so doing, putting aside lesser issues of identity and nationality, they had managed to claw together a way of life for themselves.

I decided I must seek out my home in London to find what was left of my family, and the hope that it might perhaps provide me with a way of returning to them. My new friend Hamish agreed to loan me the international monergy to get the monorail train direct from Mallaig.

The journey took four hours. The rolling stock had been converted from the trains I had known in my own day, which was a little disconcerting.

We shot across the countryside in silence, though my fellow passengers appeared to be happy enough, wired into some kind of screens. We cut our speed as we went through the old demilitarised zone, what I would have known as the Border country. And as we went I have to say I marvelled at the new cities spread out across the moors and valleys, each one – each home it appeared – designed to provide for its own energy and food needs, just as I had seen by the loch.

As we approached every border, the ticket collector went down the train checking passports and permissions from others like me without the necessary automated equipment (Hamish had given me a great deal of advice on this). Through Scotland, Northumbria, Mercia and England and on into the powerful nation known as London.

Yet this was not London that I understood. There seemed to be almost as much traffic as ever, though it was silent and clearly the air in London was certainly fresh. To my great surprise, the city centre was now a huge estuary nearly all the way up towards Kings Cross Station. The old buildings had mainly gone. It was a shock.

I had almost no luggage and I walked to my home down the Euston and Marylebone Road past the missing towers and the new buildings, like the people, designed in what was clearly a trendy

Elizabethan style. I wished I had asked Hamish where parliament now was for the FBI. Westminster was under water, or so I gathered.

Paddington was equally unfamiliar. The old towers had gone and had been replaced by the same kind of homesteads that I had seen all the way down from Scotland – small and white and clean somehow, and self-sufficient. My own home, I was relieved to see, was still standing. I knocked on the door and was staggered to find my own wife opening it.

I began suddenly, and fatally, to hope.

"Darling, I'm home!" I said, but she was clearly frightened and tried to push the door shut.

"Sarah," I shouted, desperate now. "It's me! Do you not recognise me?"

By now, I had my foot in the door and had glimpsed what I hoped to see down the hallway. There was the portrait of my wife, painted as a wedding present.

"There's some crazy guy on the other side of this door! Quick – give me a hand!" she was calling to someone.

"Don't do this to me, Sarah!" I shouted. "Look! There's a picture of you staring at me from the end of the hall, where it's always been!"

The door open slowly, revealing the woman I had taken to be my wife.

"Ohmygod!" she said. "You're talking about Sarah, my great grandmother."

These are the facts of my predicament. If you read this published anywhere and you have a proposal that I might use to get back to my own time, I would be grateful if you could contact me at +10276 Scot 307 &^%//ahfrg. Thank you so much.

Do you believe in fairies?

An essay

"Do you believe in fairies? Say quick that you believe! Clap your hands!"

Those were the crucial, and rather unexpected, words which greeted the Edwardian theatregoers in evening dress two days after Christmas 1904, at the premiere of *Peter Pan*. Surprising because they had expected another of J. M. Barrie's domestic comedies; crucial because this was the moment when the audience is asked to suspend adulthood and credulity.

Despite *Peter Pan*'s success, these are not really words you can bawl at the New York Stock Exchange or at a match between Real Madrid and AC Milan. Prevailing culture – such as it is, in recent years – has moved on from fairies, and Arthur Rackham's diaphanous things, not to mention Arthur Conan Doyle's coy photographs.

What was winsome and liberating for Barrie is now slightly nauseating to most of his great grandchildren (not that he had any). Something about the whole Tinkerbell thing – the delicate femininity, the questionable childish sexuality – did not mix well with the century to come.

Six years after Conan Doyle's faked photographs, Sir Quentin Craufurd founded the Fairy Investigation Society, designed to promote serious study. Over the years, it managed to attract a number of prominent supporters, including Walt Disney and the Battle of Britain supremo Air Chief Marshal Lord Dowding, whose career was not helped by his public expressions of belief.

But by the 1970s, the Society could stand the cynical public climate no longer and it went underground. I wrote to their last known address outside Dublin some years ago, and had a strange letter back. It was from a man claiming that he knew the society's secretary, but he said he didn't want to talk to anybody. Not only the fairies had disappeared, but the fairy researchers seem to have fled as well.

I know about this because I had the temerity to write a novel for grown-ups about fairies, with my tongue barely in my cheek at all. There was some interest from the big publishers, but only on condition that I took out the fairies. Instead, I clapped my hands – and did it through a small publisher instead (*Leaves the World to Darkness*).

Yet there is something about the beginnings of

centuries that seem to resurrect the whole idea of from utter oblivion. A century after *Peter Pan*, just when you thought it was safe at the bottom of the garden – when the whole notion of the 'little people' had been consigned to effete affectation – the idea of fairies seems to be making a comeback.

There are at least twelve major fairy festivals taking place this year, from Bodmin Moor in Cornwall to Tacoma in Washington State. In fact, to sell copies of my novel, I found myself at the first fairy festival in the UK.

It was a fascinating experience, joining nearly 400 fairy enthusiasts, of all shapes, ages, classes and genders, many of them sporting a variety of different wings – some of them also with wands and tinsel – on a damp weekend in Cornwall. Also rather peculiar. I normally exist firmly in the metropolitan world of think-tanks and politics, with the occasional foray into writing history books.

Yet there I was, near Jamaica Inn, amidst a flurry of wands, wings, long striped socks, pointed shoes, garlands of flowers and what you might call Greenpeace chic. The truth was that there was something refreshing to be there when I knew that, in Whitehall, there was the most utilitarian government since they stuffed Jeremy Bentham. Somehow, a few hours at the 3 Wishes Fairy Festival was, for me, the antidote to Tesco and BAA.

The fairy sub-culture is not happening entirely below the radar of the chattering classes. The Royal Academy ran a highly successful exhibition of Victorian fairy paintings in 1998, which went on to acclaim at the Frick in New York, the University of Iowa and the Art Gallery of Ontario in Toronto. Susanna Clarke's brilliant novel *Jonathan Strange & Mr Norrell* also has a prominent role for a fairy.

But there are also now whole orchestras of people describing themselves as 'fairy musicians'. There is a new magazine, published in Maryland, called *Fairie*, and enough new fairy websites to re-populate Google. There is even an American attempt to re-brand Midsummer's Day as 'Fairy Day'.

The key question is this. We live in a society so technocratic that we have pills to control over-exuberant boys – why, in those circumstances, are fairies staging such a comeback?

But there were some clues at the 3 Wishes Fairy Festival, and its very distinctive style – dungeons and dragons by way of Botticelli – and its array of small businesses offering music, books and spells. Festival organiser Karen Kay, a former broadcast journalist, says it's about concern for the environment. She's probably right. There does seem to be something about which not only recognises the mystery, hidden life and sheer magic of woods, forests and the natural world, but which also flies in the face of brute fact.

"A man can't always *do* as he likes," said John Ruskin in his Slade lecture 'Fairyland' in 1893, "but he can always *fancy* what he likes."

One of the problems for 20th century audiences was, of course, that Ruskin did rather fancy fairies – or at least their human equivalent. But let's leave that on one side. The point is that were for him, and maybe also for us, an antidote to grim reality.

But can we actually believe in them? There is a fascinating story of a fairy encounter in Janet Bord's book *Fairies: Real Encounters with Little People* about a strange experience reported in 1973 near Alderwasley in the Amber Valley in Derbyshire.

Suddenly, next to a grassy bank on a beautiful summer's day, there was a four-foot green man. The witness describes a short conversation, during which the fairy – if indeed that's what he was – said that his work involved breaking down decaying material for food for plants. Other twentieth century witnesses have talked about claiming that they are helping trees to grow.

I'm not saying these people were necessarily reliable witnesses for a crown court trial. Nor am I saying that I would go to the stake in defence of their sanity. But the idea appeals to me.

If are some hidden aspect of natural processes, the personification of rotting or photo-synthesis in a parallel reality, then – yes, maybe I can believe in them. Whether these processes also have some power over human luck, as are traditionally supposed to have, well – who knows.

Certainly I prefer to live in a world where there are parallel ways of looking at reality, just as there are shades of opinion, than the miserable cut-and-dried utilitarian world I seem to have been born into.

Will this admission help my career in the world of think-tanks and politics? Almost certainly not. But, when all is said and done, we do need to stand up for a bit of mystery.